Enid Blyton's

STORIES FOR
BEDTIME

Enid Blyton's

STORIES FOR
BEDTIME

Made and Printed in Great Britain by Purnell & Sons, Ltd.
Paulton (Somerset) and London

603 03263 x

CONTENTS

Mr. Stamp-About in a Fix

"I've written three time to Mr. Tiles to tell him to come and mend my roof!" said Mr. Stamp-About to his sister. "And what does he say? He says he's too busy! Pah! Too busy to mend *my* roof! Just wait till I see him!"

"Please don't stamp on that rug," said his sister. "You're making such a dust. I think it's because you're so bad-tempered that people won't come and do things for you. Now stop stamping. If you *want* to beat the dust out of that rug, take it out, hang it over the line and beat it."

"Pah!" said Mr. Stamp-About, and stalked out of the room. He put on his hat and went to find Mr. Tiles. He found him in a shed, getting together his tools to go and do a job of work.

Mr. Stamp-About caught hold of him. "Ha! I suppose you were just about to come and mend my roof! Now don't you dare to say you weren't! You come along with me this minute!"

7

Little Mr. Tiles looked at the big, fierce Mr. Stamp-About. "Let go," he said. "If you force me to go with you like this I'll have to come— but I won't put your tiles on properly, so there!"

"Oh, yes, you will!" said Mr. Stamp-About. "Because I'll sit by you and watch you! And not a penny will you get if you don't do your best work. Now bring some tiles along with you, and a pot of paint, too, to touch up the gutters. And I shall sit on a chimney-pot and watch you!"

"You will, will you?" said little Mr. Tiles. "Right. I'll get the tiles—here they are. And I'll bring this pot and this brush along with me. Off we go!"

And off they went together, Mr. Stamp-About holding on fast to Mr. Tiles in case he ran off. But he didn't. He walked along quite amiably, and talked about the weather.

"Fetch the ladder," said Mr. Stamp-About, when they got to his house. "It's in my shed. Climb up it first and begin to put on the new tiles. I'm going to have a cup of hot cocoa as it's a cold day. Then I'll come up the ladder, and sit on a chimney-pot to watch you. I'll have a fine view of your work, I can tell you!"

Mr. Tiles went to fetch the ladder. He set it up against the gutter and climbed up. Mr. Stamp-About had disappeared into the house to get his cocoa. Dear, dear—he hadn't even thought of offering cold Mr. Tiles

a cup. Still, that suited Mr. Tiles all right. He had something to do before Mr. Stamp-About came out again!

He climbed the ladder quickly, taking his tiles with him. He set them down on the roof and then went back for his pot and his brush. He grinned as he brought those up. He took a quick look down. Mr. Stamp-About was nowhere to be seen. He was somewhere in the house, having cocoa and biscuits!

Mr. Tiles looked at the two chimneys sticking up out of the roof. One was smoking. One wasn't, so that was the one that Mr.

Stamp-About would sit on to watch Mr. Tiles doing his work! Aha!

Mr. Tiles climbed up to the chimney-pot. It was squat and round. He took his brush and dipped it into his pot. He painted the rim of the pot round and round and round.

But not with paint. Oh, no! There was no paint in that pot—there was glue. Nice, sticky glue! Aha, Mr. Stamp-About, you didn't know that, did you, because the pot was labelled "White Paint"!

Mr. Tiles grinned. He slid down to where

the roof needed new tiles and set to work. Presently he heard Mr. Stamp-About climbing up the ladder. He saw him clambering up to the chimney-pot and sitting himself flat down on it, just as if it were a stool. Mr. Tiles grinned to himself.

"Now, get on, Tiles," said Stamp-About. "I can see everything you do. You're to work well and quickly. I'm not going to pay you too much, either."

"You're going to pay me five pounds," said Mr. Tiles. "Or your sister is. Five pounds, Mr. Stamp-About—part-payment for this work, and part-payment for your bad temper!"

If Mr. Stamp-About hadn't been stuck fast to the chimney-pot he would have fallen off in rage. He stamped his feet on the roof and loosened another tile.

"That's no good!" said Mr. Tiles. "That will cost you even more for another tile. Still, stamp about, Stamp-About. I don't mind your paying me more money!"

Stamp-About shouted, roared and stamped. Mr. Tiles took no notice. He finished his work and went down the ladder.

"Five pounds and five shillings!" he shouted to Stamp-About. "I'll get it from your sister as I'm sure you won't give it to me!"

Mr. Stamp-About tried to get up from his chimney-pot seat, but he couldn't. Something seemed to be holding him back. What *could* it be?

"Come back! Don't you dare to ask my sister to pay you!" he yelled. "I'll pay you one pound and that's too much!"

"Goodbye," said Mr. Tiles, jumping off the ladder. "Be careful you don't loosen any more tiles!"

He went into the house and told Stamp-About's sister she was to give him five pounds and five shillings. She took it out of the cash-box and gave it to him. He beamed and went out.

"Where's my brother?" called the sister. "I must just be certain the amount is right."

"He won't come in for a bit," said Mr. Tiles with a grin. "You can ask him then."

Off he went, looking back now and again to see the furious Mr. Stamp-About. There he sat on the chimney, trying his best to get up, but

the glue was much too strong for him. He raged and stamped and shouted, and soon a collection of interested people came to watch.

"I'm stuck, I'm stuck!" he yelled. "Get me down!"

But people were afraid of his bad temper, and, besides, they were pleased to see horrid old Stamp-About stuck up on his own chimney-pot. And will you believe it, there he had to stay till a downpour of rain came and thinned out the glue.

Poor Mr. Stamp-About. He was soaked

14

through, and he missed his footing as he climbed down the roof, bounced down the ladder, and landed with a bump on the ground.

"Stamp-About! What *do* you think you are doing, sitting on a chimney-pot, shouting and yelling like that, and then falling off the roof?" cried his sister. "I'm ashamed of you. You can go straight up to bed. I've had enough of you today!"

And you'll hardly believe it, but Stamp-About had had such a lesson that he did go straight up to bed. He never forgot his day on the chimney-pot—and neither did anyone else!

The Grumpy Goblins

ALAN was cross and tired. He had worked hard at school all day, and then when he had got home to tea, his mother had sent him out on errands until bedtime.

"I haven't done my homework!" said Alan, to his mother, when she said it was time for bed.

"Well, what homework is it?" she asked.

"I've got to think of twelve words beginning with *gr*," said Alan. "Miss Brown says the *gr* family is quite easy, and we must all come to school tomorrow ready to make sentences with words beginning with those two letters. So, Mother, I must sit down and think some out."

"Oh, you can do that in bed!" said Mother, and Alan had to go upstairs at once. He was cross, because he felt sure it would be difficult to think out homework in bed—and he was right, for no sooner was he under the bedclothes trying to think, than his mind wandered away and wouldn't even *try* to get hold of any *gr* words.

"If only somebody would tell me a few!"

thought the little boy. He opened his eyes—
and how he stared! What do you think he saw?
He saw six funny little goblins sitting on his bed-
rail, and one of them was holding a dog on a lead.
The dog was just like Alan's own toy-dog, but
he seemed to be very much alive.

"Who are you?" asked Alan, sitting up.

"We're the Grumpy Goblins," said one.

"Oh," said Alan, "I suppose you are always
cross then."

"We grumble," said one. "And we groan,"
said another. "And we grouse," said the third.

"And we *growl*," said the dog, unexpectedly, and gave a fierce growl that made Alan jump. He tried to spring down on to the bed, but the goblin pulled him back."

"Grab him!" said the others.

"He wants one of my chocolates!" said Alan, seeing the little dog sniffing in the direction of his box of sweets.

"Greedy dog!" said the goblin, who had the dog's lead. "Grubby fellow!" said another. The dog jumped back on to the bed-rail with a grunt. "He grunts like a pig," said the first goblin.

"Gracious!" said the dog's master. "Now he's grinning!" Sure enough the dog was smiling from ear to ear. Alan thought it was all most interesting.

"Do tell me why you've come to visit me," said Alan.

"Your grievance called us," said the goblins. "Though gruff and grumpy and grave, we granted your wish."

"What wish?" asked Alan, sleepily.

"Well! Where's your gratitude?" snapped the goblin. "Come, Grumpies—and gradually —gradually—gracefully—gracefully . . ."

"Gradually gracefully *what*?" said Alan, half-asleep—but the Grumpy goblins were gone! The dog jumped down on to the bed, and cuddled beside Alan. The little boy slept.

When he awoke in the morning he looked at the dog and remembered the queer goblins. "You *are* my own toy-dog, after all!" he said. "I wonder what you were doing with those goblins. Oh—I think I know—you fetched them to do my homework for me. Yes—they did it all! I can write down heaps of words beginning with *gr* this morning—and I guess I'll get top marks!"

He did. Could you?

The Girl Who Was Left Behind

"To-morrow we're going for a day by the sea, by the sea!" sang the children in Miss Williams's class.

"Well, mind you are none of you late for the motor-coach," said Miss Williams, gathering up her books. "The coach will be at the Town Hall at ten o'clock. It will wait for ten minutes only, then it will start. So you must all be very punctual!"

"We'll be there before the bus!" said Millie.

"We'll be ten minutes early!" cried John.

"I'll have to do my mother's shopping first, but I can get there by ten o'clock," said Alice.

They all went home, happy because they were to have a fine day's holiday by the sea tomorrow. Paddling, bathing, digging—what fun they would have!

All the children were up early the next day. It was Saturday. Most of them had little jobs to do. They had to make their own beds. They had to tidy up their toys. They had to feed chickens, or perhaps help with the shopping.

"I'm off to do Mother's shopping now," said Alice, peeping over the fence at Millie, who was sitting reading in her garden. "Wait for me, won't you? I'll be back as soon as I can. Then we'll run together to the Town Hall to get into the big motor-coach."

"I'll wait for you," promised Millie. "But don't be late, for goodness' sake!"

Alice set off. There was a lot of shopping to do, and the shops were full. She stood for a long time at the grocer's, but at last she was served. Then off she went to the baker's and to the greengrocer's.

She looked at a clock. Half-past nine. She must hurry home now, because she had to put on a clean frock. She would just be in nice time.

She hurried home. She gave her mother the shopping and counted out the change. She was a good, sensible little girl, and her mother trusted her with a lot of things.

Then she went upstairs to put on her clean frock. But, oh dear, it had a button off! Never mind, there was just time to sew it on. Alice got out her needle and cotton.

Soon she heard Millie coming in from next door and calling up the stairs.

"Do come, Alice. It's five to ten! Do come. I shan't wait for you."

"Coming, coming!" cried Alice, and slipped her frock over her head. She buttoned it quickly, fetched her hat and coat, and ran downstairs. She kissed her mother goodbye, and ran out with Millie.

"It's ten o'clock already," said Millie. "The

23

coach will be there. We shan't get the best seats."

They ran down the street. Just as they got to the corner a boy came round on a bicycle. A dog ran across the road, and the front wheel of the bicycle ran into him. The dog yelped. The boy fell off his bicycle with a crash, and the bicycle fell on top of him. He hit his head on the kerb and lay still, stunned for a moment.

The girls stopped in alarm. Alice ran to the boy. He opened his eyes and sat up, rubbing his head, which was bruised and bleeding.

"I feel funny," he said. "I've hurt my head. Oh, look at my poor bicycle. I can't ride it home. The front wheel is bent. And all the things are spilt out of my basket. Could you pick them up for me, please?"

He was a boy about Alice's age, but she did not know him. She began to pick up the spilt things. Millie wouldn't help.

"Alice! We simply can't stop! Let someone else help him! We've got to catch that coach!"

"You help me, then, and we'll be able to," said Alice. "You pick up the things, and I'll help the boy up. Go on, Millie."

"What, and lose the coach that is going to take us to the sea!" cried Millie. "It's five past ten already! I'm going. Are you coming or not, Alice?"

"Oh, yes, yes, just wait a minute. I can't leave this boy till he can stand up properly and wheel his bike," said Alice, anxiously. "There's nobody else about to help him. You go on, Millie, and just tell Miss Williams I'll be along in a minute. Don't let the coach go without me."

Millie ran off, looking cross. How silly of Alice to mess about like that! Let the boy help himself! He wasn't badly hurt. He could easily pick up his own things. Well, even if Alice was going to miss the coach, Millie wasn't!

She tore round the corner, and ran down to the Town Hall. Thank goodness, the coach was still there. All the other children were in it. Miss Williams was standing beside it, looking anxiously for Millie and Alice.

"Where's Alice?" she said.

"Oh, she's messing about round the corner!" said Millie, unkindly. "She just won't be quick. I did tell her we'd be late. I left her behind."

"The naughty little girl," said Miss Williams,

looking at her watch. "I'll wait one more minute, and then we shall go."

Alice helped the boy to his feet. He seemed a bit better. All his things were soon back in his basket. His bicycle could not be ridden. He would have to wheel it home.

"You sit down on that wall over there for a few minutes before you wheel your bike home," said Alice, "then you'll feel well enough. I'm sorry I can't stay and see you home, very sorry, but you see, the coach won't stop longer than ten minutes past ten."

She ran off, and the boy looked after her, thinking what a kind little girl she was. It was nice to find someone kind when you were hurt and dizzy. Kindness was one of the best things in the world.

Alice rushed round the corner, and looked anxiously at the Town Hall, which she could see from there. There was no motor-coach waiting for her! It had gone! Yes, there it was, climbing the hill beyond. It hadn't waited.

Alice stood and looked after it. It hadn't waited. Just because she had stopped to be

kind, she had missed a lovely day by the sea. Millie, who hadn't been kind at all, had caught the coach.

"But I couldn't help stopping to pick that boy up," said Alice. "I just couldn't. And now the coach has gone without me."

Tears came to her eyes and trickled down her cheek. She had hurried so much, she had done all the shopping, she had had plenty of time at the last—and yet she was left behind.

She turned to go home. She had forgotten about the boy sitting on the wall. She walked past him, her tears blinding her. She gave a little sob. She was so dreadfully, dreadfully, disappointed.

The boy saw her in surprise. Hadn't she told him she was going to catch a motor-coach? Surely it hadn't gone without her!

"Hi!" he called. "What's the matter? Come over here and tell me."

So Alice told him, and then it was the boy's turn to comfort poor Alice. "What a shame!" he said. "I stopped you from catching the coach. Oh, I do feel dreadful about it. Poor, poor Alice."

"I can go home with you now, and wheel your bicycle, if you like," said Alice, wiping her eyes. "You look rather pale, and you ought to have your head bathed. Come along."

So she took the boy home, wheeling his bicycle for him. He lived in a lovely house about three streets away. His mother was in the garden, and came running to meet him.

"What have you done, Donald? Oh, your poor head. What has he done, little girl?"

Alice told her. Then Donald told his

mother how Alice had helped him. She was so grateful.

"Come along in and have some lemonade," she said. "I'll just bathe Donald's head. I don't think it's really very bad."

While his mother was bathing his head, Donald told her how poor Alice had missed the motor-coach because she had stayed to help him.

"So there will be no day by the sea for her," he said. "And all because of me!"

His mother looked thoughtful. Then she smiled. "Alice shan't miss her day by the sea!" she said. "I will take her, and you, too, in the car! It will do you good to have a blow by the sea, after this nasty little fall. We will go to your Auntie Lou's for the day and have a lovely time! Would you like that?"

"Oh, *yes*!" said Donald, cheering up at once. "Shall I go and tell Alice? Have you finished with my head? Oh, won't she be pleased!"

Alice was. She could hardly believe her ears. After her big disappointment it seemed too good to be true that she was going to have a day by the sea after all! She thanked Donald's mother shyly, and her eyes shone with joy.

They soon set off in Donald's mother's little car. First they went round to Alice's mother and told her. She was very surprised, but pleased to know that Alice had been so kind.

Then off they went. It was a fast little car, and Donald's mother drove well. Alice enjoyed it. She had never been in a car before, and it was lovely.

"We're going so fast," she said. "Shall we pass the motor-coach that the others are in?"

"Well—they had a good start," said Donald's mother. "We may get there about the same time."

The funny thing was—they did! Just as the little car drew up on the sea-front for the two children to look at the calm blue sea, a big motor-coach drew up too—and it was the one with all the school-children in!

"*Look!* There's Alice! Surely that's Alice!" cried Millie in amazement. "Alice, Alice, how did you get here? We left you behind!"

She jumped down and ran to Alice. But Donald did not welcome her. "This is the other girl who saw me fall," he said to his mother. "But she didn't help. She just stood

and said they would miss the coach, and ran off without Alice—and she didn't even get the coach to wait!"

Millie went red. She knew she had been selfish and unkind. She went back to the others, still red. Now she wished she had been kind, too! Here was Alice, going to have a lovely day with Donald's kind mother—and going back in a car! And Millie had thought her so silly to stay behind and help.

32

Alice had a wonderful day. Donald's Auntie Lou was as kind as his mother, and they all four had a picnic on the beach and ice-creams afterwards. They had ice-creams again at tea-time, and Donald and Alice had three rides each on a donkey, and a lovely bathe.

"Now we must go home," said Donald's mother, who had been watching Alice and

thinking what a well-mannered, nice little girl she was. "Come along."

"Oh, I wish the day wasn't over!" said Alice with a sigh. "I have so loved it."

"We'll have more days like this," said Donald's mother. "You must come to tea with Donald every week. You will be a nice friend for him—someone who is kind and unselfish. Donald is kind, too, so you will make a good pair!"

They do, and they are very happy playing together. "Your bit of kindness brought you a big reward," Alice's mother said. It certainly did, but I think Alice deserved it, don't you?

The Story of Lucky

ONE day, when Mary and Jack were walking home from school, they saw a crowd of children watching something. They ran up to see what it was.

"Oh," said Jack, angrily, "look, Mary. Those three boys in the middle have got a young puppy, and they're teasing it. Isn't it a

shame! The poor little thing is terribly frightened."

"Well, no one seems to be doing anything about it," said Mary, "so *we* must. Come on, Jack, we'll rescue it."

The two children pushed their way through the others, and faced the three boys.

"Don't be so cowardly," said Jack, bravely. "Leave the puppy alone. Give it to me, and I'll take it home, if it belongs to no one. It's a shame to tease a little thing like that."

Mary caught hold of the puppy and held it tight. One of the boys pulled her hat off, but she didn't care. Another boy tried to push Jack over, but he wasn't going to run away, not he! Then some of the other children came round the puppy, and said:

"Poor little thing! Mary and Jack are quite right to rescue it. Run away, you naughty boys, or someone will catch you."

Then Mary and Jack took the puppy home, and told their mother all about it.

"May we keep it?" asked Jack. "No one owns it, Mother. What shall we call it?"

"Yes, you may keep it," said Mother. "Call

it Lucky, for really it was very lucky to be rescued by you."

So they called it Lucky. It loved Jack and Mary, and grew into a big, strong dog. They always took Lucky for walks with them, and he used to go rabbit-hunting and was very happy indeed.

One day the three of them went for a walk by the lake. Lucky tore off after a rabbit and left Mary and Jack alone. And then a dreadful thing happened. Mary was walking just at the edge

of the lake when suddenly her foot slipped, and over she went, right into the deep blue water!

Jack was frightened. Mary couldn't swim, and neither could he. He couldn't reach her, for the bank was high above the water. No one was about. What was he to do? Mary would drown if he didn't do something! Then he suddenly thought of Lucky.

"Lucky!" he shouted. "Lucky! Lucky! Come here, quick, Lucky!"

Lucky bounded up, and in a trice he saw poor Mary struggling in the water below.

Splash! In he jumped and swam to her. He caught hold of her dress in his strong teeth and swam to shore, dragging her after him. He found a place where the bank was low, and Jack helped to drag Mary out. She was gasping and spluttering, but in a few minutes she was all right again.

"Oh, Lucky!" she said, hugging him hard. "You saved my life! Brave Lucky! Good Lucky!"

"Wuff!" said Lucky, and licked her face. Then they all ran home to Mother.

"He has paid you back for rescuing him when he was a puppy," said Mother. "Hurrah for good old Lucky!" and she gave him three chocolate biscuits for a treat!

The Wind and the Seeds

ONCE upon a time there was an old woman who hated flowers. She was half a witch and lived all alone in a little humpy cottage on the hillside. Round the back-yard ran a high red wall, so that no one could look over and spy what the old dame was doing. But there was a gate in the wall and early in the morning, before the old woman was awake, her next door neighbour, Mister Twinkle, used to slip in at this gate and plant things in the ugly back-yard.

Twinkle thought that Dame Doldrums would be pleased when she saw gay nasturtiums and candytuft shining there. But she wasn't. She flew into a terrible temper and nearly turned Twinkle into a bumble-bee, but she didn't know quite enough magic.

"I won't have flowers in my back-yard!" she stormed. "I won't! I hate them! I hate anything lovely. I'm a bad old woman and I know it, but I just don't care. I'm going to wall up the gate, and I'm going to put spikes of glass and iron on the top of the wall, and a spell too,

to prevent anyone getting into the yard to plant things. And I'm going to use a spell to kill every single seed that lies in my yard at this moment! Then I shan't have a single flower! Grrrrrr!"

Twinkle fled away, frightened. Dame Doldrums did all she said. Soon there was no garden gate, and horrid sharp spikes appeared along the wall. There was a spell too that prevented anyone going within twenty feet of the wall, and every little seed in the yard was killed before it could sprout and grow.

Then Dame Doldrums shut herself up with her old black cat and began to knit a long green shawl.

The sunny days went by, and no one came near the ugly back-yard. They couldn't, and they didn't want to, either. Did I say nobody? Well, perhaps it wasn't quite right to say *no-body*, because the wind came and had a look over the wall. The wind laughs at spells and sharp spikes, and this strong west wind didn't even notice them. But it did see the empty back-yard.

"Shocking!" shouted the wind, in a gusty voice. "Shocking! Not even a blade of grass! I must put this right at once!"

On it went, hunting here and there; and you should have seen what it brought back with it! Bits of thistledown, crowds of floating dandelion parachutes, twirling sycamore keys and merry-go-round ash spinners; seeds of all sorts of daisies, big and little, fluffy tails of old man's beard, and wispy seeds of willow-herb. What else? Oh, I couldn't tell you, there were so many seeds of all shapes and sizes, all eager and ready to fly off with the wind.

Over the wall they went and settled on the empty soil. There they lay all the cold winter through, but when the warm rains of spring came, and the golden sunshine, how they sprouted! How they sent down roots and shot up green fingers! And how they flowered! The ugly back-yard was a perfect mass of bright colour, and lovely scents wafted in at the old dame's kitchen window.

She smelt them and looked out. When she saw all the gay flowers and tiny trees she gave a scream of rage and fear. She caught up her broomstick, sat upon it with her old black cat and flew straight up the chimney. Nobody knows to this day what became of her—but the wind roared with laughter so that all the biggest trees nearby shook and shivered with his roaring.

He is still at his tricks with the seeds. Have *you* seen him blowing them about?

The Sandy Rabbit's Party

Soon the Sandy Rabbit would be two years old, and he meant to have a party. He felt most excited, and rubbed his paws together in delight.

"My birthday is at the end of October!" he said. "It is now the beginning. I will send out all my invitations at once!"

So he sat down and wrote six cards in his very best handwriting, and then sent them off. They went to Slinky the Snake, Flitter the Bat, Derry the Dormouse, Prickles the Hedgehog, Crawler the Toad, and Big-One the Badger.

Everyone accepted. Parties did not come very often, and nobody meant to miss this one. Sandy Rabbit was known to be generous, and all the invited guests felt certain that they would have a fine feast.

"There will be a few frogs for me!" thought Slinky the Snake.

"There are sure to be fat flies for me!" squeaked Flitter the Bat.

"There will be hazel nuts for me and a few acorns," said Derry the Dormouse.

"Beetles and grubs for me!" decided Prickles the Hedgehog.

"A dozen bluebottle flies for me!" croaked Crawler the Toad.

"*I* should enjoy a few mice and lizards," grunted Big-One the Badger.

Sandy Rabbit knew perfectly well what all his guests liked best, and all that month he set about getting his birthday feast ready. Goodness! What a larderful he had! He hired a large table, and bought a new blue-checked

tablecloth. He knitted himself a new yellow scarf, and had his whiskers nicely trimmed. He meant to look his best, and to give the finest party that had ever been heard of!

Towards the end of the month there came a very hard frost, when the earth was frozen, and the wind was bitter. Sandy Rabbit didn't care! He grew a thicker coat, and ran about to keep himself warm. The east wind blew hard, and the trees grew bare and cold. The swallows all disappeared, and the robin fluffed out his feathers and thought it was time to go and tap at the window of the little girl he knew. He wanted some crumbs.

Sandy Rabbit was very happy. His birthday was coming near, and his lovely, lovely party! When the day came at last it was bitterly cold and Sandy Rabbit put up his big table in the shelter of the hedgerow. He spread it with all his goodies, put on his new scarf, and then looked out eagerly for his guests.

But alas! Slinky the Snake didn't come. Flitter the Bat was nowhere to be seen. Derry the Dormouse was not to be found. Prickles the Hedgehog didn't arrive. Crawler the Toad

was not there—and as for Big-One the Badger, no one had seen him for days.

Sandy Rabbit sat and cried by himself. "Nobody loves me!" he sobbed. "I expect they've all gone to someone else's party. Oh, how I wish I knew what had happened!"

Well, *I* know what had happened, and what all the guests were doing. Do you? If you do, write a note to Sandy Rabbit and tell him. He will be *so* pleased!

The Very Clever Kite

TIMOTHY was so excited. Mummy was going to take him to see a conjurer at the Town Hall, and it was said that he could really do the most marvellous things imaginable! He could put water into a teapot, and when it poured out, it was cocoa! And then by waving his handkerchief over the cup of cocoa, he could turn it into a bowl with a goldfish swimming about. Just imagine that!

So it was no wonder that Timothy was excited. He kept thinking and thinking and thinking about the conjurer, and he was so pleased and happy that he simply could *not* sit still for a moment!

It was a very windy day. The trees sang a song as they swung their branches about. The smoke from the chimneys twisted this way and that like witches' cloaks, and the flag on the flag-mast at the bottom of the garden flapped as if it had wings!

There came a knock at the door. Mummy

went to it, and there was the laundry man, with the basket of clean linen.

"Wait a moment," said Mummy. "I will pay you."

She ran to get her bag, and took a pound note out of it. Just as she was handing it to the man, a dreadful thing happened. The wind suddenly blew by in a terrific gust and snatched the note out of Mummy's hand. In a trice it was blown away, high in the air, and flew right over the hedge, and was lost to sight!

"Oh!" cried Mummy, in dismay. "Quick! Let's look for it! Timothy! Come and help!"

Well, they all hunted and hunted and hunted—but not a sign of that pound note could they see! It might have blown as far as the next village, for all they knew.

Mummy went sadly back to the house.

"Timothy, I can't take you to see the conjurer now," she said. "I am so very sorry. But I've no more money."

Timothy was dreadfully disappointed. He wanted to cry—but when he saw his mother looking so upset he knew that he must pretend not to care, so that she wouldn't feel even more unhappy. So he gave her a hug, and said "Never mind, Mummy! *I* don't mind about the conjurer! Don't you worry about *me*!"

Wasn't that nice of him? He went and put on his hat and coat to go and tell his friend Jimmy that he would not be going to see the conjurer now, and to ask Jimmy if he would be sure to remember everything to tell him, if *he* went.

"Jimmy's out in the field flying his kite," said Jimmy's mother. So

Timothy ran to the field; and sure enough, there was Jimmy, flying his kite high in the air. What a wind there was! The little boys could hardly hear themselves speak!

"The kite can't go any higher!" said Jimmy. "I've used every single inch of string!"

"I hope the string won't break," said Timothy anxiously. "The kite is pulling very hard!"

And do you know, *just* as he spoke, the string *did* break! Wasn't it dreadful? It broke a little way up in the air—and the kite at once flew away, dragging its long tail and its string behind it!

"Oh!" cried Jimmy, in dismay. "My lovely kite! It's gone!"

The two boys watched it. It dipped down suddenly, then dipped again, and disappeared behind a tree.

"Quick!" said Timothy. "We may get it if we hurry. Perhaps it is caught somewhere."

The boys raced over the field, climbed over the wall at the end, and found themselves in a little wood. They hunted anxiously for the kite, and could not see it anywhere.

"It's too bad!" said Timothy. "This horrid wind! It blew away my Mummy's money to-day so that she can't take me to see the conjurer—and now it's taken away your kite!"

They went on hunting—and suddenly Timothy gave a shout, and pointed upwards.

"Look! It's up there! Caught in that tree!"

"Oh dear! I can't

climb *that* tree," said Jimmy. "I'd be afraid of falling.

"Well, *I'll* climb it and get the kite," said Timothy. "I'm used to climbing. I'm always climbing the trees in our garden at home."

So up he went. It was very difficult. A branch caught at his leg and scratched it. A big twig stuck into his cheek and pricked him. But up he went—and at last he reached the kite. He pulled it free from the branch it had fallen on, and was just about to go down again when he saw a big hole in the tree. "I wonder if there's a nest there," he thought, and slipped his hand in.

There was a nest—but it was a very old one, falling to pieces. There was something that rustled in the nest. Timothy thought it was a dead leaf. He pulled it out to see.

But when he saw what it was he got such a surprise that he *very* nearly fell right out of the tree! It was the pound note his mother had lost! Yes, it was, really!

"The wind must have blown it all the way across the field, into this tree—and it must have slipped into the hole!" cried Timothy. "Oh, Jimmy, Jimmy, what luck! Now Mummy will be able to take me to see the conjurer after all. Hurrah!"

"Hurrah!" cried Jimmy too, pleased to see his friend's excited face. "Throw down the kite, Timothy. We'll race home and tell your mother."

They tore off—and Timothy's mother was *so* pleased and excited. She hugged both little boys, and heard the story of how the kite got caught in the tree, again, and again, and again.

"We'll go to see the conjurer and we'll take Jimmy with us, as it was his kite that so kindly found my money for me!" she laughed.

"Wasn't it a *clever* kite!" said Jimmy, full of joy to think that he was going to have such a treat.

Well, they all went to see the conjurer that afternoon, and didn't they have fun! Do you know, the conjurer took a shilling out of Jimmy's left ear, and a rabbit out of Timothy's cap. It was really most astonishing!

"I don't think I've ever seen a cleverer thing!" cried Jimmy, as they went home.

"Except your kite!" said Timothy. "That was even cleverer than the conjurer, Jimmy! It found a pound note in a bird's nest instead of an egg!"

The Elephant and the Snail

ONCE upon a time a great elephant went roaming with the herd in the forest. As he went between the trees, pulling down leaves and fruit to eat, a snail fell off a nearby bush, and went rolling to where the elephant stood.

It was a fine snail, with a big, curly shell, brightly coloured in yellow and brown. It rolled underneath the great foot of the elephant. The big beast felt it rolling there, and lifted his foot to see what it was.

When he saw that it was only a snail, the elephant put down his foot again, meaning to crush the snail—but the tiny creature spoke earnestly to the elephant:

"Don't crush me! Put down your foot to one side and let me crawl away in safety. I have never done you any harm, so have mercy on me, great elephant."

The elephant was not cruel. He moved his enormous foot away and looked at the yellow and brown snail.

"Well, go in peace," he said. "I will not harm you."

"You are a kind creature," said the snail gratefully, moving away. "One day I may be able to save your life for you in return."

The elephant trumpeted loudly with laughter. "How could a creature like you ever do anything for me?" he bellowed. "You think too much of yourself, snail!"

The snail said no more, but slid away as fast as it could for fear the elephant should change his mind and step on him. He hid in the bushes until the herd had gone by. All small creatures feared the heavy tread of the elephants.

The weeks went by. Hunters came to the wood—men who wished to capture the elephants and set them to work. They built a big enclosure of strong fences with a wide entrance.

"Now," they said to one another, "we know where the herd is. We will surround it and drive it gradually to our enclosure. The elephants will all go inside—and then they will find they cannot get out. They will be caught!"

So the next day the hunters went out to surround the herd. But the elephants were very wary and they had moved off—all except three who were separated from the herd. They were

caught, for they ran when they heard the hunters coming, and very soon they had lumbered into the big ring of fencing, and were prisoners.

The three elephants trumpeted in rage. They knew they were caught. They tried to rush out of the gateway—but now the big gate had been closed, and there was no way out. The elephants pushed against the fence, but it was too strong to break down, even when the three of them pushed together. A fence like that would need a whole herd to push it down!

The elephants bellowed with anger, but they could do nothing. One of them was the elephant who had let the snail go free, but he had forgotten all about the little creature by now.

But the snail had not forgotten. When it heard the bellowing of the elephants, it crawled from its hiding-place nearby, and glided up to the top of the fence. On the other side stood the elephant the snail knew so well!

"Friend!" said the snail. "Why do you roar so loudly?"

"Because I am caught," said the elephant sulkily. "I cannot get away from here."

"Can I help you?" asked the snail.

The elephant laughed. "Of course not!" he said. "What can a snail like you do, I should like to know? Can you break down this fence? Can you open the gate? No—you are a worthless little snail, and can do nothing!"

"Could your friends help you?" asked the snail.

"Yes, if they were here," said the elephant. "But they do not know where I am. If the whole herd were here they could easily knock down this fence. But before they come wandering by this way again I and the other two elephants here will be taken away."

"I think I *can* help you," said the snail. "I know I crawl very slowly, but if you would tell me where to find your friends, I might be able to get to them in time for them to come here and break down the fence for you."

The elephant stared at the yellow and brown snail in surprise. "You are kind, snail," he said. "But you are such a slowcoach that it would take you weeks to crawl to my friends."

"I will try," said the snail. So the elephant told him where he thought the rest of the herd would be, and the little snail crawled down the fence again and made his way through the forest grass.

Certainly the snail was a slowcoach, but he did not rest for a moment. He kept a sharp eye for birds, and went on his way steadily. He glided along all night, leaving a silvery trail behind him. He slid along all day, and all the next night too. He was very tired by the middle of the second day; but to his delight he thought he heard the sound of elephants' feet thudding along not far off. He crawled up a tree and waited. Perhaps the herd was coming that way.

It was! As the leader passed the tree on which the snail hung, the little creature called to him:

"Great elephant! I have a message for you."

"Tell me," said the elephant.

"Three of your friends are caught in a big ring of fences," said the snail. "They cannot break the fence down. But if you take the whole herd there, you can break it down between you."

The leader of the elephants spoke to the

herd, and they listened, their eyes wise and bright.

"We will come where you lead," they said.

"Snail, crawl on to my head, so that you can tell me the way," said the leader of the elephants. He pressed close to the tree, and the snail dropped to his head. He clung there, and the elephant moved off.

"Who would have thought that I would ride on an elephant's head at the head of a herd," thought the little snail, astonished. He told the

63

elephants the way to go, and to his surprise they arrived near the fencing before nightfall.

"When it is dark," said the leader, "we will all go to one part of the fence. We will run against it with all our might and break it down. Keep close by me and, when I trumpet once, charge with me. Snail, crawl down from my head, for you may get hurt. You have been a good friend to us today."

The snail crawled down and glided to a thick bush. It waited there in excitement. Before long there came the sound of a trumpeting noise —and the herd of elephants charged together at the great fence.

It went down as if it were made of cardboard. The herd turned and fled, and with them went the three elephants who had been captured, overjoyed at being free again!

The hunters were astonished. "Now, who could have told the herd about the captured elephants?" they cried. "How did the herd know where they were?"

"I could answer your questions," thought the yellow and brown snail. "But I won't! It is good to help a friend!"

The elephant was grateful to the little snail. "I am sorry I laughed at you," he said. "I did not guess, when I gave you your life, that a little thing like you could help *me*!"

"Little things are very useful sometimes," said the snail as he glided away.

THE SNOW

Softly, softly falls the snow
   From the heavy sky;
Like white feathers from a dove
   Come the snowflakes from above
On the ground to lie.

Softly, softly falls the snow
   Covering hill and dale,
Till the world is strangely fair,
   White trees gleaming everywhere
Like a fairy-tale!

The Little Toy Stove

ANGELA had a little toy stove. It was a dear little stove, with an oven that had two doors, and three rings at the top to put kettles or saucepans on. At the back was a shelf to warm plates or keep the dinner hot. Angela did like it very much.

But Mother wouldn't let her cook anything on her stove. "No, Angela," she said; "you are not big enough. I am afraid you would burn yourself if you lighted the stove and tried to cook something."

"Oh, but Mother, it isn't any fun unless I can cook myself something!" said Angela, nearly crying. But Mother wouldn't let her light the stove, so it was no use saying any more about it.

Now one day, as Angela was playing with her saucepans and kettles in the garden, filling them with bits of grass for vegetables, and little berries for potatoes and apples, pretending to cook them all for dinner, she heard a tiny voice calling to her.

"Angela! Angela! Do you think you would

mind lending me your stove for this evening? My stove has gone wrong, and I have a party. I simply *must* cook for my guests, and so I wondered if you'd lend me *your* stove!"

Angela looked all round to see who was speaking. At last she saw a tiny elf, not more than six inches high, peeping at her from behind a flower.

"Oh!" said Angela in delight. "I've never seen a fairy before. Do come and let me look at you."

The elf ran out from behind the flower. She was dressed in blue and silver, and had long shining wings and a tiny pointed face. Angela thought she was lovely.

"Will you lend me your stove?" asked the elf. "Please say yes."

"Of course!" said Angela. "I'd love to. Will you really cook on it? My mother won't let me."

"Of course she won't let you," said the elf. "You aren't big enough yet. You might burn yourself."

"Shall I leave my stove here for you?" asked Angela.

"Yes, please," said the elf. "I can easily cook out here. It is to be an open-air party. I live behind these big hollyhocks, so I shan't have far to bring my things."

"I suppose I couldn't come and watch you?" said Angela longingly. "I've never seen my toy stove really doing cooking, you know!"

"Well, you come and watch to-night," said the elf. "I shall begin my cooking at nine o'clock. The party begins at eleven."

Angela was so excited when she went in to

bed. She meant to put on her dressing-gown and get up at nine o'clock, and creep down the garden. So she lay awake until she heard the hall clock chime nine. Then up she got and slipped down the stairs and out of the garden door.

She could quite well see where her toy stove was, because smoke was rising from it. The elf had got it going well. A lovely smell of baking and roasting came on the air. Oooh!

You should have seen the elf cooking on that stove. The oven was full of things roasting

away well. The saucepans were full of delicious fruits and vegetables!

"This stove cooks very well indeed," said the elf, pleased. "It's a fine stove. Just listen to my pudding boiling away in that saucepan."

"What sort of pudding is it?" asked Angela.

"It's a tippy-top pudding," said the elf. "And I'm cooking a poppity cake too and some google buns."

"Oh my, they do sound delicious," said Angela; "and so exciting! I've never heard of them before. I suppose I couldn't come to the party?"

"No," said the elf. "It is too late a party for little girls like you. But, Angela, as I think it is really very kind of you to let me use your lovely stove for my cooking, I'd like you to taste some of my dishes. Listen! There is sure to be some tippy-top pudding, some poppity cake, and a few google buns over after the party. If there are I will put them on a plate and leave them inside the oven. See? I will clean the stove nicely too, and leave it all shiny and bright. Now, good-night, dear. You must go to bed. You are yawning."

"Good-night!" said Angela, and she ran off. In the morning she went to see if there *was* anything inside her oven. And what do you think? There was a neat little blue dish, and on one side of it was a slice of yellow tippy-top pudding, and on the other side were three google buns, red and blue, and a large slice of green poppity cake! Ooooh!

Angela ate them all—and they were simply delicious. She *does* so hope that the elf will want to borrow her stove again. Wouldn't it be lovely if she did?

Amelia Jane is Terribly Naughty

ONCE Amelia Jane, the big naughty doll, discovered a tiny hole in the eiderdown on the dolls' cot.

So she poked her finger inside and pulled out a feather. She threw it up into the air.

"Look!" she shouted. "This eiderdown is full of feathers. Did you know there were feathers in eiderdowns, Toys?"

"Amelia Jane! Don't pull out any more feathers!" said the golliwog at once, seeing the big doll pull out two more.

"Oh, I must, I must," said Amelia, and she tore the hole a little more till it was quite a big one. Then she could put in her hand—and out came dozens of feathers!

"I shall make a snowstorm, a snowstorm, a snowstorm!" sang Amelia Jane in delight. She climbed up on to the nursery table and began to shake the eiderdown. Well, as you can imagine, out flew hundreds and hundreds of white feathers! Amelia Jane became very excited.

"I'm making snow, I'm making snow!" she shouted. "Come out into the snowstorm, Toys!"

The toys stared at the naughty doll in dismay. What a mess she was making! Whatever were they to do? The feathers flew all about the room, floating lightly in the air—and you know, it really did look rather like a snowstorm.

Amelia Jane got another eiderdown—and she made a hole at one end. She climbed up to the table again and shook the eiderdown. Out flew hundreds more feathers!

She squealed with delight. "You'll soon be able to make a snowman, Toys!"

"Don't be so silly, Amelia Jane," said the

clockwork clown. "I simply can't *think* how you can be so naughty."

"Oh, it's quite easy," said bad Amelia Jane, and she shook twenty feathers down on the clockwork clown's head. The clockwork mouse watched from a corner. He really felt a bit afraid of so many feathers.

"I wonder where there is another eider-down," said Amelia Jane, who never could stop, once she had begun. "Oh, I believe I know where there is an old cushion. That will be full of feathers too. I think I saw one of the children put it on the top shelf of the nursery cupboard. I'll climb up and see."

She went to the cupboard, walking through the cloud of feathers. She blew them away as she went. It was fun. She came to the cupboard and opened the door. In the cupboard were many shelves, for a great deal was kept there—the nursery cups and saucers were there, the knives and forks, the medicines, the treacle for the porridge, the honey, the jam, a tin of biscuits, mending things—and on the top shelf was a collection of things that needed sewing—a cush-ion with a hole in, a tea-cloth, and a tablecloth.

Amelia Jane began to climb up the shelves—and then a dreadful thing happened. She caught hold of the saucer in which the tin of treacle stood—and it tipped up at once. The lid came off—the treacle tin lost its balance and fell straight on Amelia Jane's head. The treacle trickled down all over her.

"Ooooh, Amelia Jane! *Now* look what you've done," shouted the toys, as they saw the treacle dripping down all over the big doll.

"Oh! I don't like it! It's sticky!" cried

75

Amelia Jane, and she jumped down from the cupboard.

And then a funny thing happened. The feathers which were still floating all over the room, fell on to the sticky treacle—and before you could say, "Look at Amelia Jane!" she was covered with feathers!

The toys began to laugh. They simply couldn't help it. First Amelia was covered with treacle, and then with feathers—and it was all because of her own naughtiness!

"*Don't* laugh at me, you horrid things!" yelled Amelia in a temper, and she ran at the toys. But the more she ran through the feathers, the more stuck to her—and at last she looked like a strange and peculiar bird!

The toys laughed till they couldn't laugh any more. Amelia Jane got angrier and angrier, and tried to tear off the feathers. Then she lay down on the floor and rolled about to get them off— but she forgot that there were hundreds of feathers on the carpet, so when she got up there were more stuck to her than ever!

"It's the funniest sight I've ever seen," said the golliwog, wiping his eyes, for he had laughed till he cried. Amelia Jane caught up a stick and ran at the golliwog. She hit him hard. Then she hit the teddy-bear and then ran at the frightened clockwork mouse. She was a big doll and could hit very hard indeed. The toys were really terrified, but Amelia wouldn't stop.

"*I'll* teach you to laugh at me!" she cried.

And then something happened to Amelia. The door of the nursery opened softly, and in walked the big black kitchen cat. When he saw Amelia Jane, covered in feathers, he stopped and stared.

"What! A *bird* in the nursery!" he mewed. "I'll catch it for my dinner!"

Then it was Amelia's turn to be frightened. She ran into a corner and hid there. "No, don't catch me, don't catch me!" she cried. "I'm Amelia Jane!"

"Rubbish!" said the cat. "You've got feathers growing on you—dolls don't have feathers! I shall catch you, you most peculiar bird!"

He crept quietly up to the corner. Amelia gave a squeal and ran away. She hid behind the brick-box. The cat followed again, and crouched down, ready to spring. Amelia yelled for help.

"Toys! Save me! Save me! Quick, come and help me!"

But the toys thought it was time that Amelia was punished. She had hit them all very hard— now she must see what it was like to be chased and hurt.

The cat sprang. He landed right on Amelia Jane and squashed all the breath out of her. He dug his claws into her and scratched her. She squealed and squealed.

The cat sniffed at her in disgust and then

78

jumped away. He couldn't bear the sticky
treacle on his paws. He licked them clean and
then walked out of the nursery with his tail in
the air.

"You're only a doll after all," he said.
"Well, if you dress yourself up in feathers and
treacle, you must expect trouble!"

Amelia Jane cried so much that the toys
came round to comfort her. She had had her
punishment, and they were too kind-hearted
to keep away any longer.

"Now listen to me, Amelia," said the golliwog sternly. "We will wash the treacle off you

—but after that you must see to the feathers. You must pick up every single one and stuff them all back into the eiderdowns, and sew up the holes. Do you hear?"

"Yes, Golly," said Amelia Jane in a small voice. So they took her to the basin and washed away the treacle. It made her very wet and she had to dry herself by the fire. Then she had to pick up all the feathers. Nobody helped her, because, as the golly said, she really had to learn that she must pay for being naughty.

Then Amelia Jane put the feathers back and sewed up the holes in the eiderdowns. "I've done all you said," she said in a sorry sort of voice. "I won't be bad again."

But nobody believed her—and I don't expect you do either!

The Two Cross Boys

Tom and Willie were cousins. Sometimes they went to stay with one another, and that was fun —at least, it *would* have been fun if they hadn't quarrelled so much!

The worst of it was that when they quarrelled they wouldn't make it up, and, of course, that's very silly. But Tom's mother cured them, as you will see.

Willie went to stay with Tom, and for the first two days they had a grand time. Tom was so pleased to have Willie to play with that he let him have all his toys.

"You can ride my tricycle if you like!" he said. "You can bang my drum when you want to. You can climb that tree down there in the garden that I call my very own."

"Thank you, Tom," said Willie, and he rode the tricycle, beat the drum, and climbed the tree.

And then, after two days, they quarrelled. Quarrels are often about silly little things that don't really matter at all, and this one was so silly that you will hardly believe it.

Tom hit his elbow hard against the wall and it hurt him. The tears came into his eyes. Willie saw what he had done and he laughed.

"You shouldn't cry, Tom," he said, "you should laugh! That was your funny-bone you hit against the wall."

"It was not a funny bone at all," said Tom, who didn't know that we call the point of our elbow our funny-bone. "It wasn't a bit funny. It was horrid. I'm hurt."

"Well, if you don't laugh at your funny-bone *I* shall!" said Willie teasingly. "Ha ha ha! Ho ho ho!"

"You horrid thing!" said Tom angrily. "You shouldn't laugh when people are hurt. I shan't speak to you!"

"Funnier than ever," said Willie. "Ha ha ha! Ho ho ho!"

Tom slapped him. Willie slapped back. Then they both yelled at the tops of their voices, for Tom had slapped Willie on the cheek and Willie had slapped Tom on the nose, and both places hurt.

Tom's mother came hurrying out. "Now, now," she said, "quarrelling again! I did think that this time you were old enough to play nicely together. Shake hands and make up your quarrel, and then go and dig in the sand-pit in the field, for a treat."

"I don't want to shake hands," said Tom, and he turned away.

"I shall never speak to Tom again," said Willie as Tom marched off with his hands in his pockets, and his nose looking quite red from the slap it had received.

Tom's mother went indoors again, thinking what little sillies the two boys were. "I expect they'll soon get over it," she thought.

But, you know, they didn't! They wouldn't smile at one another or speak to each other all day. They wouldn't say good-night at night. They wouldn't sit next to each other at break-fast-time the next morning. It was very un-pleasant for Tom's mother, for she did like smiling faces and happy talk.

"What are you going to do this morning?" she asked.

"Well, if Tom's going to be in the garden I shall be indoors," said Willie sulkily.

"And if Willie's in the house I shall be out-side," said Tom at once.

"You are both very silly, stupid boys," said Tom's mother. "You are wasting all the time you have together just because you can't make up a quarrel about Tom's funny-bone."

"I'll do any jobs for you, Auntie," said Willie, feeling a bit ashamed of himself. "Give me some work to do and you'll soon see I'm not stupid."

"If anybody's going to do a job for my

84

mother, *I'm* going to do it!" said Tom at once.

"Well, you shall *both* do a job for me," said Tom's mother, and she smiled a funny little secret smile to herself.

"What is the job?" asked Tom.

"I want the big kitchen window cleaned," said Tom's mother.

"Well, Mother, I said if Willie's in the house I shall be out-of-doors," said Tom. "I won't work in the same place with him."

"Very well," said his mother. "You shall clean the inside of the window and Willie shall clean the outside. I've got two window-leathers, so that will be all right."

In a little while the boys went to do their job. Each had a brown window-leather, damped with water. Tom was to do the inside, and Willie was to do the outside of the window. Each of them was quite determined to do his side better than the other.

They began. They wouldn't look at one another, but Tom thought it would be fun to pretend to rub out Willie's red face. So he rubbed hard with his leather just where Willie's face was. And then Willie guessed what he was doing, and he decided he would rub out Tom's face!

So he ducked down to see Tom's face, and then began to try to rub him out through the glass!

Now you can't do things like this without feeling rather giggley. It's funny to begin with, to rub away so near to one another, with only the window in between—and it's funnier still if you are cross and try to rub someone out!

Then the boys found that their hands were rubbing in time, together—forward, back, one, two; forward, back, one, two! Then they rubbed fiercely at one another's hands—and then they caught one another's eye, and found that each had a little twinkle in it!

"I shan't look at him," thought Tom. "If I do I know I shall laugh."

"I won't even peep at him!" said Willie to himself. "I feel as if I shall giggle if I do!"

But they did keep looking at one another just to see if the other was smiling—and soon Tom's mouth curled itself upwards, and he had to hide it in his handkerchief. And then Willie felt as if he was going to giggle, swallowed the

giggle, and choked and spluttered till he was
scarlet in the face!

He looked so funny that Tom began to
giggle too. He tried to stop. He shut his
mouth. Another giggle burst out of it. He ran
away to a corner of the room, put his head into a
cushion and laughed till the tears came out of his
eyes and trickled down the cushions.

Willie peeped through the window and saw
what Tom was doing, and that made him laugh

87

too. He sat on the window-sill and roared with laughter.

Tom's mother heard them and looked into the room. "Whatever are you laughing at, Tom?" she asked.

"Oh, Mother, it's so funny to clean a window with somebody else cleaning it outside," said Tom. "I just can't help laughing."

Mother went outside. "What *are* you laughing at, Willie?" she said.

"Oh, Auntie, you should have seen Tom and me cleaning this window together!" he giggled. "Tom tried to rub me out and I tried to rub him out—it was so funny."

"Show me how funny it was," said Mother, and she called Tom. Then the two boys showed her, giggling as they rubbed their leathers to and fro across the window, grinning at one another. Mother laughed and laughed.

"Yes, it's very funny," she said. "Now would you both like to run down to the sweet-shop and share a pennyworth of sweets together for doing my window so nicely?"

Now you can't go on quarrelling with somebody you've giggled with. Every time Tom looked at Willie he laughed, and Willie kept giggling too.

"Yes, we'll go together," said Tom. "Shake hands, Willie. Let's be friends again. I can't laugh with an enemy!"

"Nor can I!" said Willie. So they shook hands and were friends. Mother gave them a penny and they went off to buy the sweets. On the way Willie was rather thoughtful.

"What's the matter?" asked Tom.

"I'm just thinking about your mother," said Willie. "She's really very clever, Tom. She *knew* we would laugh over cleaning the same window—she knew we would try to rub each other out. It was her way of making us friends! Didn't I giggle too! I nearly choked with trying not to!"

Wasn't it a fine idea of Tom's mother? Now when the boys quarrel she looks at them and says, "Do you remember how you cleaned that window together?"

Then they giggle, of course, and everything is all right again!

Poor Captain Puss!

DONALD and Jill were very lucky. In the summer they always went to Cliffsea, where their father had a house almost on the beach. It was such fun to wake up in the morning and hear the waves splashing on the sands not far off.

All the household went to Cliffsea in the summer, even Toby the dog, and Patter the kitten! No one was left behind. Toby liked the sea very much, and Patter loved playing about in the sand.

Next door to the children's house was a smaller one, and two cats and a dog lived there with their mistress. The dog was called Spot, and the cats were called Sooty and Snowball, so you can guess what they were like to look at.

Toby, Patter, Sooty, Snowball, and Spot were soon good friends. Patter the kitten had a fine time with them. They made quite a fuss of her because she was the smallest and youngest.

So she was rather spoilt, and she became vain and boastful. Ronald and Jill spoilt her too, and said she was just the cleverest kitten they had ever seen.

"See how she runs after my ball!" said Ronald, as Patter raced over the sand to get his ball.

"See how Patter plays with this bit of sea-weed!" said Jill. "She fetched it off the rocks for me, Ronald. She *is* a clever kitten! She can do simply anything!"

Patter felt very clever indeed. She went about with her head in the air and began to think that the other animals were rather stupid.

But there was one thing she would *not* do! She wouldn't go paddling and bathing with the

children as Toby and Spot did. No—she hated
the water. She thought it was simply horrid
to get her dainty little feet wet.

Then one day Ronald and Jill brought down
a beautiful big ship to the beach. It was a toy
one, but was so big that Toby or Spot could
almost get into it. Ronald and Jill played happily
with it all the morning, and sailed it on the
rock-pools that were spread all over the beach.

When they went indoors to dinner the five
animals crowded round the pretty boat.

"I wish I could sail in it!" said Toby. "I'd

love a sail over that pool. I would make a good captain!"

"So would I," said Spot, wagging his tail and sniffing at the boat as it stood half-upright in the sand.

"I would make the *best* captain!" said Patter the kitten boastfully. "Ronald and Jill are always saying what a clever kitten I am. I am sure I could sail this ship much better than any of you!"

"Why, Patter, you little story-teller!" cried Snowball, "you know how you hate to get your feet wet! You wouldn't be any good at all at sailing a boat."

"Yes, I should," said Patter crossly. "I know just what to do. You pull that thing there—the tiller, it's called—and the boat goes this way and that. I heard Ronald say so!"

"You don't know anything about it at all," said Sooty scornfully. "You are just showing off as usual!"

"I'm not!" mewed Patter angrily. She jumped into the boat and put her paw on the tiller. "There you are," she said. "This is what makes the boat go!"

The others laughed at her. They were sure that Patter would hate to go sailing really. They ran off and left her. She stared after them crossly, and then she lay down in the boat in the warm sunshine. She wouldn't go and play with the others if they were going to be so horrid to her. No, they could just play by themselves!

Patter shut her eyes, for the sun was very bright. She put her nose on her paws and slept. She didn't hear the sea coming closer and closer. She didn't know the tide was coming in! It crept up to the boat. It shook it a little. But Patter slept on, dreaming of sardines and cream.

Toby, Spot, Sooty, and Snowball wondered where Patter was. They couldn't see her curled up in the ship. They thought she had gone indoors in a huff.

"She is getting to be a very foolish little kitten," said Toby. "We must not take so much notice of her."

"It is silly of her to pretend that she would make such a good sailor," said Sooty. "Every one knows that cats hate the water."

"Well, we won't bother about her anymore," said Snowball. "She's just a little silly. Let's lie down behind this shady rock and have a snooze. I'm sleepy."

So they all lay down and slept. They were far away from the tide and were quite safe.

But Patter was anything but safe! The sea was all round the ship now! In another minute it would be floating! A great big wave came splashing up the beach—and the ship floated! There it was, quite upright, floating beautifully!

The rock-pool disappeared. It was now part of the big sea. The ship sailed merrily on it. It bobbed up and down on the waves.

Patter suddenly woke up, and wondered

why things bobbed about so. She sat up and saw that she had fallen asleep in the boat—and when she looked over the side, what a shock for her! She was sailing on the sea! Big waves came and went under the boat. The beach was far away!

"Miaow!" wailed Patter. "Miaow! I'm out at sea! I'm afraid! I shall drown!"

But no one heard her. The sea was making such a noise as the tide came in. Patter forgot how she had boasted about being a good sailor.

97

She forgot that she had boasted she could sail the boat quite well. She just clung on to the side and watched with frightened eyes as the green waves came and went.

Ronald and Jill suddenly remembered that they had left their sailing ship on the beach.

"My goodness! And the tide's coming in!" said Ronald in dismay. "Quick, Jill, we must go and see if our boat is safe!"

They ran from the house to the beach—and then saw that the tide was right in. And, far away, on the big waves, floated their beautiful ship, all by itself!

"Look!" cried Jill. "There it is! But there is someone in it. Who is it, Ronald?"

Ronald stared hard. Then he shouted out in surprise: "Why, it's Patter the kitten! Yes, it really is! Look at her in the boat, Jill!"

"Oh, the clever thing!" cried Jill, who really thought that the kitten was sailing the ship. "Oh, whoever heard of a kitten sailing a boat before! Spot, Toby, come and look at Patter sailing our ship!"

Spot, Toby, Sooty, and Snowball awoke in a hurry and ran to see what all the excitement

was about. When they saw Patter the kitten out in the boat, rocking up and down on the sea, they could hardly believe their eyes.

"Captain Puss is sailing the boat," said Jill. "Captain Patter Puss! Isn't she clever!"

But Spot didn't think that Patter was as clever as all that. His sharp ears had caught a tiny mew—and that mew was very very frightened. It wasn't the voice of a bold captain—it was the mew of a terrified kitten!

"I believe she went to sleep in the boat and the tide came and took it away," wuffed Spot to Toby.

"Well, it will do her good to see that she isn't such a marvellous captain after all!" Toby barked back.

"She *would* be silly enough to fall asleep just when the tide was coming in," said Sooty.

"All the same, she's very frightened," said Snowball, who had heard two or three frightened mews.

"Sail the boat to shore, Patter!" shouted Ronald. "Sail her in! We don't want to lose her!"

But Patter was much too frightened to pay

any attention to what was said. She just went on clinging to the side of the boat. She felt very ill, and wished that she was on dry land.

Spot was quite worried. He knew what a little silly Patter really was—but all the same he thought she had been frightened quite enough. What could be done?

"I'll go and fetch her," wuffed Spot, and he plunged into the sea. He swam strongly through the waves, which were now getting quite big, for the wind had blown up in the afternoon. Up and down went Spot, swimming

as fast as he could, for he was really rather afraid that the ship might be blown over in the wind—and then what would happen to Patter!

The boat was a good way out. The wind blew the white sails strongly. The waves bobbed it up and down like a cork. Patter was terribly frightened, for once or twice she thought the boat was going over.

And just as Spot got there, the wind gave the sails such a blow that the boat *did* go over! Smack! The sails hit the sea, and the boat lay on its side. Splash! Poor Patter was thrown into the water. She couldn't swim—but Spot was there just in time! He caught hold of her by the skin of her neck, and holding her head above the water, he swam back to shore. The ship lay far out to sea on its side.

Spot put poor wet, cold Patter on the sand, and shook himself. Patter mewed weakly. The others came running up to her.

"Well, you didn't make such a good sailor after all," said Sooty.

"Don't say unkind things now," said Snowball. "Patter has been punished enough. Come

into the house, Patter, and sit by the kitchen fire and dry yourself."

Ronald and Jill watched the five animals running into the house. Then Ronald turned up his shorts and went wading into the water to see if he could get back his boat.

"That kitten was silly!" he said. "She took my boat out to sea, couldn't sail it back again, made it flop on to its side, and fell out herself! She isn't so clever as she thinks."

He got back his boat and went to dry the

sails in the kitchen. Patter was there, sitting as close to the fire as she could, getting dry.

"Hullo, Captain Puss!" said Ronald. "I don't think you are much of a sailor!"

"No, she is just a dear, silly little kitten," said Jill.

Patter felt ashamed. How she wished she hadn't boasted about being a good sailor! She wondered if the others would ever speak to her again.

They did, of course, and as soon as they found that she wasn't boastful any more they were as good friends as ever.

But if Patter forgets, they laugh and say, "Now, Captain Patter! Would you like to go sailing again?"

Simon's Clean Handkerchief

"MOTHER," said Simon one day, "the teacher says I *must* take a clean handkerchief to school each day."

"Good gracious me, I should think so," said his mother. "You know where your clean handkerchiefs are, don't you, Simon? Well, just see you take one each morning."

So the next morning Simon started off with a nice clean handkerchief. He was so pleased to have it that he carried it in his hand. He meant to show it to his teacher as soon as he got to school.

But on the way Simon had to climb over a stile. He laid his handkerchief carefully down on the top and climbed over. And will you believe it, he left his handkerchief on the stile. When he got to school the teacher said, "Did you remember your handkerchief today, Simon?"

"Yes," said Simon—but, dear me, it wasn't in his hands and it wasn't in his pockets. "I've left it on the stile," said Simon. "Bother!"

As he came home from school he looked for

his handkerchief—and there it was on the ground, in rags! Daisy the cow had come along and seen it on the stile. She had given it a chew and then spat it out. It was no use at all as a handkerchief now!

That afternoon Simon took another handkerchief from his drawer. "I will tie a knot in it to remind myself to hold on to it all the way to school," he thought. So he tied a big knot in the corner. Then off he went.

He climbed over the stile safely, his handkerchief in his hand. He went on jogging along happily. Suddenly he saw a butterfly and he went after it. It settled on a flower. Simon put down his handkerchief, and crept up to the butterfly. He pounced—but the butterfly was gone, flying high into the air!

"Bother!" said Simon, and skipped off to school. He had left his clean handkerchief on the ground!

"Where is your handkerchief, Simon?" asked the teacher.

"Oh," said Simon proudly, "do you know, Miss Brown, I tied a knot in it to remind me to bring it! Wasn't that clever of me!"

"Well, where is it?" asked Miss Brown.

Well, of course, Simon couldn't find it anywhere! He had left it behind on the grass.

Miss Brown was cross with him.

"You are a naughty little boy," she said. "Now just remember it tomorrow, please."

So the next morning Simon took another handkerchief from his pile. He hadn't been able to find the one he had left on the grass, because the wind had blown it away.

"Now I really and truly will remember to

take my handkerchief this time!" said Simon. "I will not let it leave my hand all the way to school."

Just as he started off, his mother called him. "Simon, dear! Post this letter for me on your way, will you?"

"Certainly, Mother!" said Simon. He took the letter and ran off. He wondered if he remembered his six times table, because he knew Miss Brown was going to hear it that morning. So he began to say his tables:

"Six times one are six,
Six times two are twelve."

As he was saying his tables he came to the pillar-box, red and shining in the roadway. He ran up to it, saying his tables all the time, and was proud to think he knew the whole of six times. But do you know what he did? He posted his handkerchief instead of his mother's letter! Oh, Simple Simon, whatever is any one to do with you!

"Well, Simon," said his teacher, as he ran into school. "I hope you've got your handkerchief today!"

"Yes, Miss Brown," said Simon proudly. "I kept it in my hand all the time—look!"

He handed her—his mother's letter! Miss Brown stared in surprise.

"But this is a letter, not a handkerchief, Simon," she cried.

"Oh my, oh my!" groaned poor Simon, looking at it. "I must have posted my handkerchief! Yes—that's what I did!"

"Simon, I shall be very cross with you soon," said Miss Brown. "Please do try to bring a clean handkerchief this afternoon. I will give you one more chance."

So Simon once more took a clean handkerchief from his drawer that afternoon. He put it into his pocket. He thought it would be safer there than in his hand! Off he started to school. But on the way he fell down. His knee bled, and his hands were covered with mud. Poor Simon! He took out his handkerchief and scrubbed his hands. He wiped his knee. Then on he went again. But it was not Simon's lucky day. He brushed against some wet paint, and his nice jersey was covered with blue! Out came the handkerchief again, and Simon wiped off the blue paint.

But he did arrive at school with his handkerchief, and proudly he showed it to Miss Brown.

"Simon! What is that horrid, dirty, smelly rag!" she cried. "Surely it is not a handkerchief! Didn't I say you were to bring a *clean* handkerchief? Just see you do tomorrow morning, or you will be spanked!"

Simon cried all the way home, and when he told his mother what had happened she was cross with him. And she was crosser still when she found that he had lost his hat that morning too!

"Simon, you are the silliest child I ever knew!" she cried. "Now, look here—this is one of your father's handkerchiefs, for you have used all yours. As you have no hat and the sun is very hot I am going to knot each corner of the handkerchief and make a cap for you out of it. You will wear it to school, and, goodness me, surely you can't lose it if you've got it on your head." Simon was pleased to have a

handkerchief cap. His father's handkerchief was big and red with white spots. He felt very grand going to school with such a fine red cap on.

But, bless us all, when he got to school, he had forgotten that he had the handkerchief on his head! When Miss Brown asked him to show her his clean handkerchief, Simon turned out his pockets. But there was no handkerchief there!

"Simon!" said Miss Brown, in an angry voice, "do you mean to tell me you've forgotten again!"

"No, Miss Brown," said Simon. "I *did* bring a handkerchief with me this time, I really did! But, oh dear, wherever is it?"

"Take off your cap and come indoors and be spanked," said Miss Brown, looking very cross.

Simon took off his red cap—and no sooner had he got it in his hands than he saw that it was his father's nice clean red handkerchief!

"Miss Brown, Miss Brown, here it is!" he cried. "I was wearing it on my head—and it's quite clean. Look!"

"Well, if you aren't just the silliest little boy!" said Miss Brown. "You've only *just* saved yourself a spanking! Now, in future, Simon, ask your mother to *pin* a clean handkerchief to your jersey each day—then perhaps you will be able to bring it safely to school, and I shall see it!"

So that is what Simon does now—but today his mother was away, so Simon found the safety-pin to pin on his handkerchief—but, oh dear, he made a mistake, and pinned on to his jersey the baby's best white coat. Whatever will Miss Brown say?

A Shock for Lucy Ann!

Lucy Ann was a perfect nuisance. She was always putting her nose into other people's business, and interfering in other people's affairs.

"Oh, go away, Lucy Ann!" the children said, when she tried to show them how much better it would be to do things her way and not theirs. "You are always interfering!"

"Oh, run away, Lucy Ann!" her mother would say, when Lucy Ann came poking round, telling her mother that this corner was not dusted, and that picture was hanging all crooked. "I don't need you to come poking your nose everywhere! I can see dusty corners and crooked pictures for myself!"

"Oh, Lucy Ann, please go home!" said Mrs. Brown, who lived down the road. "I don't need *you* to tell me that my garden needs weeding, and that my roses need watering. You are always putting your nose into things that are no business of yours. Go away!"

Lucy Ann frowned and went away. But she didn't stop putting her nose into everything.

She made herself such a little nuisance that no one wanted her with them.

One day, as she was coming home from school, she went across the fields. As she came near to the stile, she heard voices talking, and she looked about to see where they came from. To her surprise she saw four little men sitting under the hedge, making daisy chains. But they were not making them in the way that Lucy Ann made them! Instead of stringing the stalks together, they were threading the daisies through their heads.

"Oh!" said Lucy Ann, poking her nose into their play at once. "That's wrong! You shouldn't thread daisies that way! You want to do them like this!"

She snatched the daisies out of the hands of the surprised little men, and began to make holes through their stalks with a pin. The men jumped to their feet in anger—and then Lucy Ann saw that they were brownies. She stared at them, for she had never seen brownies before.

"You nasty, interfering little girl, poking your nose into our affairs!" cried one. "Your nose wants seeing to—it's much too sharp!"

"Let's make it sharper still, so that when she goes about interfering and putting her nose where it isn't wanted, she'll always know!" cried the smallest brownie. He reached out his bony little hand and smacked Lucy Ann sharply on the nose.

"When you poke yourself here,
And poke yourself there,
Just grow longer and sharper
And make people stare!"

cried the brownie at the top of his voice.

"Oh!" cried Lucy Ann in a rage, for the slap hurt her. She was just going to slap the brownie back when there came a puff of smoke from somewhere that hid the four little men— and when the smoke cleared away, the brownies had vanished.

Lucy Ann went home, very angry. Silly little men! She had only tried to show them the right way to make a daisy chain.

Just as she was nearly home she saw two boys she knew, playing marbles on the pavement. She stopped to watch.

"Oh, you silly!" she said to one. "You will never win if you play like that. This is what you should do!"

As she was speaking, a curious thing happened. Her nose grew very long indeed and very sharp. It poked itself among the marbles!

"Look! Look!" screamed the two boys, in fright. "Look at Lucy Ann's nose! It's like an elephant's trunk!"

Lucy Ann shrieked too. It was dreadful to feel her nose waving about like that! She ran home crying loudly. But by the time she was indoors her nose had gone back to its right size again, and her mother laughed at her when Lucy Ann told her what had happened.

But she didn't laugh when she saw it happen again! And it soon did. It was when Lucy Ann's mother was busy reading a letter. Lucy Ann came and peeped to see what was in the letter, for she simply couldn't keep out of anything!

"Who's it from?" she said—and, dear me, just as she said that her nose shot out again, long and sharp and waving, and patted itself on to the letter.

Lucy Ann's mother gave a shriek. "Oh!"

she cried, "how dreadful you look, Lucy Ann! Whatever has happened to your nose?"

Lucy Ann began to cry again. She told her mother about the brownies, and her mother nodded and frowned.

"Yes, you offended the little folk," she said, "and they punished you. Now your nose will always grow long and sharp whenever you poke it where it isn't wanted. Oh, Lucy Ann, what a dreadful, dreadful thing! You had better

come with me to old Mother Eleanor's. She knows a bit about magic and may put it right for you."

So, crying bitterly, Lucy Ann went to Mother Eleanor's with her mother. But when Mother Eleanor heard what had happened, she laughed.

"I *could* take the spell out of her nose in a jiffy!" she said. "But I shan't!"

"Oh, but what will poor Lucy Ann do!" cried her mother.

"Do?" said Mother Eleanor. "Why, keep it right herself, of course! It only grows long and sharp when she pokes it where it isn't wanted, doesn't it? Well, if she stops poking her nose into everything it won't grow long and wave about like that!"

Lucy Ann went home with her mother, and thought hard. Her nose would never be cured —unless she cured it herself! She had better try. She wouldn't interfere with any one. She would be sensible and say nothing, even when she badly wanted to poke her nose in some-where!

Poor Lucy Ann! It wasn't so easy as she

thought! Every day her nose shot out long and sharp, and every day people screamed at her or laughed loudly. But at last she tried so hard that a whole week went by and her nose stayed its right size and shape. And then she forgot again and out it shot, long and sharp, sticking itself here and there!

Lucy Ann was ashamed. She tried hard again—and, do you know, she hasn't let her nose grow long for more than a year now! She has gone to a new school, where the children don't know anything about the spell in her nose. I do hope she doesn't poke it where it isn't wanted again—because those children *will* be surprised to see what happens, won't they?

Connie's Curious Candle

THERE were four children in Connie's house. There was Philip, who was the eldest, and Helen, who was next, and George, who was seven, and then there was Connie, who was six.

There was no electric light and no gas in Connie's house. It was a very old house, and Mother used oil-stoves to cook with, and oil-lamps to light the rooms, and candles in candlesticks to light the bedrooms at night.

Each child had its own candlestick. Philip's was green, Helen's was red, George's was blue, and Connie's was yellow. Mother used to buy coloured candles, and it was Connie's job to fit the right colours into the right candlesticks.

Every night the candles were put on the hall-chest, ready for the children to carry upstairs when they went to bed. The candles used to wait there, longing for the time to come when they might wear a little yellow flame for a hat. They lighted up the bedrooms then, and they could see the children getting undressed and the shadows jumping, and they could hear the

prayers the children said and the creak when they jumped into bed.

One day Connie had to take the old bits of candle out of the coloured candlesticks and put in fine new candles. Mother had bought them that day—green, red, blue, and yellow—one for each of the children.

"A red candle for a red candlestick," said Connie, and she stuck the red candle firmly into the candlestick. "A green candle for a green candlestick. A blue candle for a blue candlestick. And here is my lovely yellow candle for my yellow candlestick. It is the prettiest of all!"

The yellow candle was pleased to hear that, but the others were not. "Yellow is a silly colour," said the red candle. "Red is the best— it is the colour of warm fire!"

"No, blue is the best. It is the colour of the spring sky," said the blue candle proudly.

"Ah, but green is the colour of the trees and the grass," said the green candle. "Every one loves green."

"Yellow is the colour of the sun," said the yellow candle timidly. "Surely that is a good colour?"

Nobody took any notice of the yellow candle at all, so he didn't say any more. He just longed and longed for the night to come so that he might wear his flame-hat and see the shadows jumping around him as he burnt.

But before the night came the children's mother came bustling into the hall, carrying an oil-lamp which she set down on the floor not far from the chest.

"It's so cold to-night I really must warm the hall," she said to Connie. "The hot air will rise up and warm the stairs too. It's bitterly cold to-day."

The oil-lamp burnt clearly and sent a yellow light over the dark hall. Connie sat on the bottom stair and watched it. There was a golden pattern on the ceiling, thrown by the lamp, and she liked it very much. She shivered. It was really a very cold day. She got up and went nearer to the lamp, holding out her doll to warm its toes. She did not go too near, for Mother had told her that oil-lamps were dangerous, and she must never go really close.

Connie looked at the candles on the chest. Her yellow one was right at the back.

"Poor yellow candle!" she said. "You must be cold, tucked away there at the back. I'll move you forward a bit and then you will be warm."

So she moved her yellow candle in its yellow candlestick, and placed it right at the front of the chest. It could almost see down into the oil-lamp! It was most exciting to watch the flame flickering up and down.

"Connie, Connie! Come out of the cold hall," called Mother, and Connie ran into the parlour where a big fire was burning. The candles were left alone in the hall, watching the golden light from the oil-stove.

Soon the yellow candle began to feel a little queer. He was hot. He felt soft. He couldn't hold his head up! He wanted to lean over to one side! It was very strange.

He did his best to stand up straight. He tried his hardest to hold firmly to the candle-stick at the bottom—but he couldn't. Slowly, slowly he began to bend himself. He dropped to one side. He curled over. He grew so soft at the bottom that he seemed to be sitting on the candlestick instead of standing in it. It was dreadful!

Of course, it was the heat from the stove that was melting him! He didn't know that, and he felt very much ashamed to think he was behaving so queerly.

The other candles began to laugh at him.

"Look at Yellow!" said Red. "He can't stand up!"

"Do you want an arm-chair to rest yourself in?" cried Blue cheekily.

"Poor old fellow! He's as bent as the old

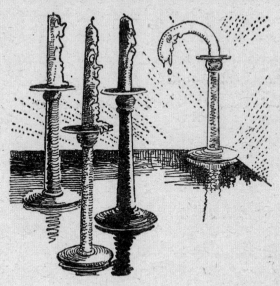

man who came begging at the door to-day,"
said Green.

"I can't help it," said Yellow sadly in a soft,
melting sort of voice. "It isn't my fault!"

"Pull yourself together!" said Red. "You
will be no use as a candle if you stand like that!"

"How can anyone light a wick that is
pointing downwards instead of up!" cried Blue.
"Why, you'd burn yourself up at once!"

"Don't frighten me," said Yellow sadly, and
he bent himself just a little more.

127

"You must be a very feeble, weak sort of candle," said Green. "Cheap, I should think. We cost threepence each. I should think you only cost a penny."

"I didn't!" cried poor Yellow. "I cost threepence, too!"

"Cheap candle!" cried Red, delighted.

"Penny candle!" cried Green, and he waggled his wick and laughed.

"Connie will throw you away into the dustbin when she sees what a useless candle you are!" cried Blue. "You won't like that. You'll have to make friends with potato peel, empty tins, and tea-leaves!"

"Don't talk to me like that," begged Yellow, and he wept two yellow tears of wax on to the chest.

Now very soon it was Connie's bedtime. She was the youngest, so she went first, at six o'clock. She danced out into the hall with Philip. He was ten, so he was allowed to light candles. He struck a match to light Connie's for her.

He gave a shout of surprise. "Look! Look at Connie's candle! It's all curled over! It's no use at all!"

Red, Green, and Blue chuckled to themselves, and poor Yellow wept another yellow tear on to the chest.

Mother came out into the hall. "Oh, Connie dear!" she said. "Did you move your candle to the edge of the chest? You have put it so near the oil-stove that it has almost melted it, poor thing! It's of no use now."

Connie looked at her candle. She couldn't bear to see it like that. "Poor candle!" she said, almost crying. "I only put it there to get warm.

Now look what I've done to it! Poor little yellow candle!"

She began to cry. Mother picked up the candlestick and looked at the curved candle.

"Connie!" she said. "Don't cry! This is a very clever candle! It knew it belonged to a little girl called Connie—and it has made itself into a beautiful letter C, for Connie. Look! It's just as good a 'C' as you do in your writing-book!"

All the children were now in the hall, and they looked at the yellow candle. Sure enough, Mother was quite right—the candle was a big curved "C"! Connie was simply delighted.

"Mother! Do you suppose a candle ever did that before?" she cried. "I shall keep it always! I shall show it to all my friends!"

"Can I put *my* candle near the stove to see if it will make the letter H?" asked Helen at once.

"Oh no," said Mother. "We mustn't waste candles like that. Connie, get the old candlestick from the kitchen, and find yourself another candle. You may take this clever yellow one to your room and stand it on your mantelpiece!"

Well, think of that! Red, Blue, and Green could hardly believe it! So Yellow was clever! Yellow was going to live on Connie's mantelpiece for a long, long time! Long after they had burnt themselves right down to the candlestick and were thrown away, the yellow candle would still stand on the mantelpiece and be admired by every one!

"It's a mistake to laugh at people!" said Red.

So it is, isn't it! Connie's yellow candle still makes a "C". I'd really like you to see it.

Mr. Twiddle and his Wife's Hat

ONE day Mrs. Twiddle wanted to take her hat back to the hat-shop because she didn't like the red roses in it.

"I would much rather have violets in my new hat," she said to Mr. Twiddle. "Don't you think violets would be nicer than roses, Twiddle?"

"Well, dear, hollyhocks and sunflowers are very beautiful too," said Mr. Twiddle, looking out into his garden proudly, where his hollyhocks were flowering very tall and straight, and his giant sunflowers were growing as high as the house, though they were not yet out.

"Twiddle! Do you think I shall put hollyhocks and sunflowers into a *hat*!" cried Mrs. Twiddle. "Do, for goodness' sake, think what you are saying!"

"I *was* thinking," said Mr. Twiddle, offended. "And I think that sunflowers and hollyhocks are——"

"All right, all right!" said Mrs. Twiddle quickly, because she didn't want to hear it all again. She took up her new hat with red roses.

"You don't think it would be nice to have a bird's wings in my hat instead of flowers, do you?" she asked.

"No, I don't," said Mr. Twiddle, who was very fond of birds and hated to see them in people's hats. "Why don't you have rats' tails or something like that? Rats are horrid things. I wouldn't mind seeing their tails in your hat at all."

"Twiddle, don't be horrid," said Mrs. Twiddle. "You know how afraid of rats I am. I should run miles if I had their tails on my head."

Twiddle thought it would be fun to see fat little Mrs. Twiddle run miles. He began to think how he could get some rats' tails for her. But Mrs. Twiddle didn't give him any time to think.

"I shall go back to the ship now," she said. "You come with me, Twiddle, there's a dear, and you shall help me to choose new flowers for my hat. You can carry the hat-box for me, too. That will be a great help."

"Very well," said Twiddle. He watched Mrs. Twiddle put her hat carefully into a box full of white tissue paper.

"You tie the box up for me, Twiddle, whilst I go and get ready," said Mrs. Twiddle. Off she ran, and Twiddle looked round for some string. There was none in the string-box, of course. There never was. Twiddle thought he had some in the wood-shed outside, so out he went.

Now when the kitchen was empty, Mrs. Twiddle's big black cat walked in. He simply loved playing with paper of any sort, so when he saw the white tissue paper sticking out of the hat-box he ran over to it at once. He pulled at it, and the lid fell off. That made him jump. He

crouched back, and then sprang at the box. He landed right inside it, on top of the hat.

"Mee-ow-ee-ow!" said the cat, pleased. It began to play with one of the red roses. It burrowed right underneath the white paper. It had a simply lovely time!

Mr. Twiddle was a long time finding the string. The cat played with the roses till it was tired. Then it settled down inside the hat, with all the tissue paper on top of it. It tucked its nose into itself and went to sleep. It loved sleeping on paper.

Presently Mrs. Twiddle bustled into the room, all ready to go out. She called Twiddle. "Twiddle, Twiddle! What in the world are you doing? I'm ready to go."

Twiddle came running in with a large piece of string. "I've been hunting for string," he said. "Really, this is a dreadful house for string. Never a bit to be found!"

"Well, hurry and tie up the hat-box," said Mrs. Twiddle impatiently. "You always take such a time over everything!"

Mr. Twiddle put the lid on the box quickly. He tied it up firmly. He fetched his hat and stick, picked up the box, and set off after Mrs. Twiddle, who was already walking down the garden path.

The box felt very heavy. Surprisingly heavy, Mr. Twiddle thought. He simply couldn't understand it. How brave women were to wear such heavy hats on their heads! He began to puff and pant.

"Twiddle! What *are* you puffing like that for?" cried Mrs. Twiddle in surprise. "It's not such a hot day as all that, surely!"

"Your hat is so heavy," said poor Mr.

Twiddle, who didn't know he was carrying a very large cat as well as the hat.

"Twiddle! How can you say that my little straw hat is heavy!" said Mrs. Twiddle. "What a fuss you do make! I'm ashamed of you."

Mr. Twiddle went redder than he already was. He hated Mrs. Twiddle to be ashamed of him. He took the box in both arms and panted along. But really, it was frightfully heavy.

"I shall have to have a rest, dear," said Twiddle when they came to the seat by the bus-stop. "This box is so very heavy, really."

"I hate stopping here," said Mrs. Twiddle. "The bus-seat is just outside the fish-shop, and I don't like the smell."

But Twiddle meant to have a rest, so he sat down, putting the box on his knee to leave room for other people on the seat. Mrs. Twiddle sat down too. She turned up her nose at the smell of the fish in the fish-shop.

The cat woke up when it smelt the fish. It was very fond of fish. It thought it would be fine to taste some, so it began to wriggle round the box to find a way to get out.

Mr. Twiddle was rather alarmed. The box

seemed to be coming alive! It moved on his knee. It shook and wriggled. Mr. Twiddle held it tightly, for he really thought it was going to jump off his knee.

"What's the matter *now*, Twiddle?" said Mrs. Twiddle, noticing that Mr. Twiddle looked frightened.

"Well, my dear, your hat is not only very heavy but it seems to be walking round the box," said poor Mr. Twiddle.

"*Walking round the box!*" cried Mrs. Twiddle.

138

"Whatever will you say next? You know perfectly well that a hat can't walk round a box."

"It seems to be *jumping* up and down in the box now," said Mr. Twiddle, beginning to tremble. The cat was doing its very best to get out. It said a few tiny mews.

"The hat is talking," said Mr. Twiddle. "I'm glad it's not *my* hat. I wouldn't wear a heavy, talking, walking, jumping hat like this for anything!"

The cat suddenly went quite mad and began to leap round and round the box, scratching at the paper as it went. Mr. Twiddle couldn't bear it any longer. He threw the box into the road!

Mrs. Twiddle jumped up with a scream.

"Oh, my new hat, my new hat!" she cried, and she ran to get it. She picked up the box and took it back to the seat. It *did* feel very heavy. It *did* feel as if the hat was leaping about. How very extraordinary! Mrs. Twiddle undid the string with trembling fingers and took off the lid.

Out leapt the big black cat with a howl, scratched Mrs. Twiddle on the hand, and flew off down the road with its tail straight up in the air!

"Was that a cat or my hat?" wept poor Mrs. Twiddle, putting a hanky round her hand.

"It was your cat," said Mr. Twiddle, glaring after the running animal. "That cat! It's always getting into mischief. Now perhaps you will say you're sorry to me, for making me carry your cat such a very long way!"

"Well, perhaps you'll say you're sorry to *me* for putting a cat into my hat-box, and letting it sit on my new hat!" sobbed Mrs. Twiddle, taking a very squashed hat out of the box. "It's chewed the roses!"

"I shan't say I'm sorry, but I'll buy you some new violets for the hat," said kind Mr. Twiddle, who was upset to see his wife so unhappy. "Come along."

"Well, I shan't say *I'm* sorry then, but I'll buy you a kipper for your tea," said Mrs. Twiddle, wiping her eyes.

So Mrs. Twiddle had her violets and Mr. Twiddle got his kipper—but, as I dare say you will guess, the big black cat got nothing at all except a good slap when he came in to sniff at the kipper!

Bertie's Blue Braces

BERTIE was very proud and pleased. His face shone, and he smiled from ear to ear.

He had on his first pair of braces! His mother had bought them for him in a real man's shop, and he had put them on for the first time that day. He had to button two buttons at the back, and four in front, where the braces divided themselves into two pieces.

"Now you are a proper man," said Mother. "You wear braces like Daddy!"

"Thank you, Mother," said Bertie, and he went out to play. His braces were under his jersey and he felt them every now and again. How grand it was to wear braces like a man! Bertie longed to show them to everyone, but he didn't quite like to.

The children played "He," and Bertie was the "He." He ran after the others, but he couldn't seem to catch anyone at all. He panted and puffed and grew very hot.

"Dear me!" he said at last. "I'm so hot I think I'll take off my jersey!"

Bertie was so pleased he had thought of that, because, you see, he knew that every one would

see his new braces then. So off came his jersey, and all the boys and girls saw his dark-blue braces.

"Ooh! You've got braces!" cried John, and he ran up to look at them.

"I say! Look at Bertie's braces!" cried Harry.

"Bertie, you *are* grown-up! I've never had a pair of braces yet!"

Everybody felt the braces and thought they were marvellous. Bertie felt as grand as could be.

"My mother says I am a proper man now," he said, "and I certainly do feel different today— sort of strong and powerful."

The other children stared at him, and thought it must be fine to wear braces. All the boys made up their minds to ask their mothers to buy them braces the very next day.

"Hie, all of you!" cried a merry voice suddenly. "Come along and play in the pits! I'm going there with Peter."

It was Willie calling. The pits were great fun to play in. They were in a field, and were a collection of big and little holes that the children loved to jump up and down in, and to hide in when they played hide-and-seek. So off they all went after William and Peter.

There was one pit that was dangerous. It was very deep indeed, and although at the top its sides did not slant very deeply, lower down they were very steep, and no child was allowed to play in that pit.

But that morning Peter felt daring. "I'm going into the deep pit!" he cried. "Who's coming with me?"

Before anyone could stop him he had

jumped into the forbidden pit. He only meant to give the others a shock, of course! But, dear me, the slanting sides of the pit began to crumble under Peter's feet and suddenly he found himself falling, falling, falling!

He clutched at an old bush and held on to it. "Help me! Help me!" he shouted. "This bush won't last long. It is breaking now! Help! Help!"

The children ran to the top. "Where's a rope?" shouted William. But there wasn't one anywhere. "What can we do, what can we do?" said Mary, looking all round for a grown-up. But not a man or woman was anywhere about.

"There's water at the bottom of that pit," sobbed Ellen, Peter's little sister. "Oh, save Peter—do, do save him!"

Then Harry thought of Bertie's new braces. "Bertie! Your braces! They would just about reach Peter if you take them off and reach down to him," said Harry.

"What! My new braces!" cried Bertie. "Oh, I couldn't use those!"

Then he saw Peter's frightened face in the pit below, and he knew he must do what he could. He threw off his jersey again, and un-buttoned his new braces. He took them off and lay down flat at the top of the pit.

"Hold my legs and feet hard, you others," he said. "I don't want to go in head-first!"

So they sat on his legs to keep him safe, and Bertie reached out his arms and dangled his new blue braces down to Peter. "Catch hold!" he

said. "I'll be able to pull you up, with the help of the others."

Peter caught hold of the end of the braces. Then John and William helped to pull him up—and at last he reached a place where he could get a firm foothold and could climb out by himself. He was very white and frightened.

"Thanks, Bertie," he said. "Sorry about your braces—we've split them—look!"

They were badly split. Bertie was sorry, and he put them on again in silence. He didn't like

147

them any more. They would hardly hold up his trousers. His mother would be cross.

"Peter, you're the silliest boy I ever knew to do a thing like that," said William. "You know we're not allowed in that pit. Now you've given us all a fright, and spoilt Bertie's new braces. I think you're just silly!"

Peter went red. He knew he had been silly. He wished he hadn't spoilt Bertie's new braces. He didn't say a word more, but ran home quickly. He told his mother all that had happened. He was very, very glad to think that Bertie had had on braces that morning.

"But they're spoilt now," said Peter. "Mother, if I weed your garden every day for two weeks, will you give me some money to buy Bertie another pair of braces? Perhaps the other children will be friends with me again if I do that—and anyway, I'm very sorry for Bertie. He was so pleased with his new braces."

"Very well, Peter," said his mother. "I will give you the money now—and you shall do my weeding for two weeks. It's the best thing you can do to make up for your silliness."

So Peter went to the man's shop and bought

a pair of red braces for Bertie. They were very grand indeed. You should have seen Bertie's face when he undid the parcel and saw them!

"Oh, Peter!" he said. "They're *much* nicer than my other ones. Thank you very much indeed."

So now Bertie wears red braces, grander even than his own father's. But I think he deserved them, don't you?

OLD CAW-CAW

The rook sits up in the old elm-tree,
And looks as wise as a rook can be,
He opens his beak, so bare and strong,
Meaning to sing us a wonderful song,
But all he can say,
Try as he may,
Is caw—
   Caw—
      Caw!
The whole of the day!

One Little Match

LITTLE Hop-Around had a small motor-car that he could pedal down the streets and back. All the other pixies thought it was a lovely thing to have.

When Hop-Around was in a good temper he let the others have rides, sitting beside him in his little car. And then one day his mother thought of a very good idea.

"Hop-Around—why shouldn't you use your

car to fetch my shopping for me? And to take
the washing to Dame Wash-a-Lot? And to
carry the potatoes we grow? What a good idea!"

Well, at first Hop-Around thought it was a
fine idea, too. He pedalled off each morning to
the shops, and brought back butter and milk
and bacon and cakes in a big basket that sat
beside him in his little car.

He took the washing to Dame Wash-a-Lot
in a big bundle. He put sacks of potatoes beside
him and went to deliver them to Mr. Fruity at
the greengrocer's.

But after a bit he didn't like doing all these things any more. "I have to pedal so hard," he told his mother. "The things I take are so heavy—especially the potatoes. My legs begin to ache when I get to the bottom of the road—and, oh dear, when I have to go up a hill with the potatoes I pant and puff like a railway train!"

"We'd better buy some wings for your car, then!" said his mother, with a laugh. "Then your legs would get a rest, Hop-Around, and you could just press a button for the wings to take your car up into the air!"

Hop-Around stared in excitement. "Ooooh! I never thought of that! Wings for my car! Could I really? I'll buy some today."

"They cost three gold pieces," said his mother. "You'll have to save up for them."

"But I'll never, never save up all that money," wailed Hop-Around. "Oh—*I've* got a fine idea, now. Mother, will you buy me some wings for the car for my birthday—instead of the big toy aeroplane I wanted?"

"Yes. I'll begin saving now," said his mother. "And you must save, too. Perhaps by the time your birthday comes we shall have enough to buy the wings, Hop-Around."

"Red wings to match my red car," said Hop-Around. "Ooooh—won't everyone stare when I fly up in the air and rush along to the shops over their heads!"

He began to save his pennies, and his mother saved her sixpences. Hop-Around would have been able to save more pennies than he did if he hadn't been quite so disobedient! There were times when he simply *wouldn't* do what he was told.

He wouldn't weed the garden because he said there were too many weeds. He wouldn't stop scribbling over his books, which was a great pity because he spoilt them so. He wouldn't remember to wipe his shoes on a muddy day.

So his father stopped a penny here and a penny there, and Hop-Around was cross because he couldn't get as many to save up as he wanted to.

"Well, it's your own fault," his mother said. "You should do what you're told."

Now one afternoon Hop-Around had a

friend to tea. His mother popped her head round the playroom door and had a look to see if they were all right. "I'm just going next door for a few minutes," she said. "Be good!"

"Of *course*," said Hop-Around, and he and Flibberty watched his mother go out of the front garden and into the one next door.

"We're alone!" said Hop-Around, excited. "What shall we do? Let's be naughty!"

"Turn on the bath-water and float your boats in it!" said Flibberty. "Or get a brush and try to sweep the chimney. Or get a tea-tray and slide down the stairs. Or——"

"You're thinking of too many things," said Hop-Around, frowning. "Let *me* think of one. Oooh—*I* know. Matches!"

"Are you allowed to play with matches?" said Flibberty. "I'm not."

"Nor am I. We won't exactly *play* with them," said Hop-Around. "We'll just use *one* match to light something with. And I know what we'll light!"

"What?" said Flibberty.

"We'll get some newspaper and stuff up the funnel of my toy engine," said Hop-Around.

"Then we'll get just *one* match and light the paper. And we'll give the engine a tremendous shove and send it round the floor with smoke shooting out of its funnel, just like a real train. It *will* look fine."

"Oh, yes! Let's do that," said Flibberty. So Hop-Around got the box of matches. He took one out and put it ready. Then he stuffed a rolled-up piece of newspaper into the funnel of his toy engine.

"Now for the smoke!" he said, and he struck the match on the side of the box. It

flared up at once. Hop-Around held it to the paper in the engine-funnel. It lighted well.

"Now give it a good shove!" cried Hop-Around. "Quick!" They both pushed the engine hard. It rolled off on its wooden wheels, smoke and flames pouring from its funnel. It looked very, very real.

But the two pixies had given the engine such a push that it ran right across the room to the window, where pretty curtains hung down to the ground, blowing in the wind. The flames from the funnel caught them—and whoooosh! a big flame shot all the way up the curtains, and smoke came from them, too! The flame from the curtain reached out to a table-lamp nearby, and the lamp-shade caught light at once and flared up with a crackling noise.

"Oh! Quick! Look what's happened!" yelled Hop-Around in a fright. "Get some water!"

But when they got back from the bathroom with a jug of water, both curtains were burnt to bits, and the lamp-shade was, too. The wooden funnel of the engine was on fire, and the engine was slowly burning away!

Splash! The pixies threw the water on the flames. Sizzle-sizzle-sizzle! They went out, and smoke rose up instead.

The door opened and Hop-Around's mother looked in. "I'm just back," she said. "Whatever is that smell of burning? Hop-Around! What's happened? Where are the curtains—and oh, that lamp-shade!"

Hop-Around was crying and so was Flibberty. "My engine!" wept Hop-Around. "It's burnt! We only took *one* little match, Mother—and look what's happened!"

The two pixies got into terrible trouble. They were both spanked, and Flibberty was sent home crying. Then Hop-Around's mother looked at him sternly.

"Your father won't pay for a new lamp-shade and new curtains," she said. "*You'll* have to pay for them, Hop-Around. You'll have to give up all the pennies you've been saving to buy wings for your car."

"I've only got twenty-two," wept Hop-Around. "You can have those."

But, dear me, when the bill came in for a new lamp-shade and new curtains, it was for far more than twenty-two pennies! It was for thirty-two shillings!

"What can I do?" said poor Hop-Around. "Will my father be very, very angry? Oh, Mother, can the bill wait till I've saved up enough to pay it?"

"No. Of course not," said his mother. "Bills must always be paid *at once*. You know that. Now, let me see—I have a lot of sixpences saved up to help to buy wings for your car when your birthday comes. I'll see how many I have. We could use those to pay the bill."

"But, Mother—I won't be able to have the wings then," said Hop-Around, dolefully.

"And whose fault is that?" said his mother. "Now let me count my sixpences. One, two, three——" and she counted them all out carefully.

"I've got exactly sixty," she said. "Now just work that out, Hop-Around. There are two sixpences in every shilling—so how many do we want for thirty-two shillings?"

"Just double," said Hop-Around. "Oh dear—we want sixty-four sixpences, and you've only got sixty."

"But you've got twenty-two pennies," said his mother. "That makes four sixpences all but tuppence. You put your pennies to my sixty sixpences, and all we need to pay the bill is tuppence more. Is that right?"

Well, if you work it out as Hop-Around did, it *is* right. Hop-Around looked very, very gloomy.

"All my pennies gone," he said, "and two more to earn. My engine burnt. All the sixpences you saved up gone, too. And no wings for my car on my birthday."

"Yes," said his mother. "That one little match cost you a lot, didn't it, Hop-Around? It's really not worth while being disobedient, is it? I'm very sorry—but I'm afraid there won't be any wings for your car *this* year."

So Hop-Around still has to pedal uphill and downhill with heavy loads beside him in his little car, and he thinks he'll have to for a very long time.

One little match! It's surprising what a lot of trouble can come from quite a tiny thing, isn't it?

The Walkaway Shoes

"You know, the two new brownies who have set up a shop in Toadstool Cottage make the most beautiful shoes," said Pixie Light-Feet to Limpy the gnome. "You should get them to make you a pair of shoes for your poor old feet, Limpy. Then you could walk well again."

Limpy went to see the two brownies, Slick and Sharpy. They bowed and smiled and welcomed him.

"Yes, yes, Limpy. We will make you such a comfortable pair of shoes that you won't want to take them off even when you go to bed!" they said.

Well, they made him a red pair with green laces, and they were so beautiful and so comfortable that Limpy went around telling everyone about them.

Soon all the little folk of the village were going to Slick and Sharpy for their shoes, and the two brownies worked hard the whole day long. They were pleased.

"Our money-box is getting full," said Slick. "Is it time we did our little trick, Sharpy?"

"It is," said Sharpy. "Now, in future we put a walkaway spell into every pair of shoes. Don't forget!"

Dame Shuffle came that day and ordered a pair of blue boots. "We've got just what you want!" said Slick, showing her a pair. "Try them on!"

She tried them on, and they fitted her so well that she bought them at once, grumbling at the

price. "I'll wrap them up for you," said Sharpy, and he took them into the other room to find some paper. He slipped a little yellow powder into each boot and then wrapped them up and took them to Dame Shuffle. Off she went, and wore them out to tea that afternoon.

"Beautiful!" said Mother Nid-Nod. "I'll get a pair from Slick and Sharpy, too."

"So will I," said Mr. Tiptap. And the next day off they went to buy a pair each. But on the way they met Dame Shuffle, who looked very worried.

"Someone came in the night and stole my boots," she said. "My beautiful new boots that cost so much. They are quite, quite gone."

"Oh dear—robbers must be about," said Mr. Tiptap. "I shall be very careful of mine when I get them."

He got a pair of red shoes and Mother Nid-Nod got a pair of brown shoes with green buckles. Slick and Sharpy grinned at one another when both customers had gone.

"Did you put the walkaway spell in them?" said Slick.

Sharpy nodded. "Yes, both pairs will be

back again to-night!" he said. "And we'll put them into our sack ready to take away with us when our money-box is quite full."

That night the spell inside Mother Nid-Nod's brown shoes and Mr. Tiptap's red ones began to work. Mother Nid-Nod heard a little shuffling sound and thought it was mice. She called her cat into her bedroom at once.

"Cinders," she said, "catch the mice in this room while I am asleep." So Cinders watched —but instead of mice running about he saw Mother Nid-Nod's shoes walk to the door, and all the way downstairs, and hop out of the open kitchen window. How scared he was!

Mr. Tiptap's shoes did exactly the same thing. The old man didn't hear anything, he was so sound asleep. But the brown owl in the woods suddenly saw a pair of red shoes walking along all by themselves, and was so surprised that he almost fell off the branch he was sitting on.

"Who-who-who is that?" he hooted. "Is there someone invisible walking in those shoes? Who- who-who is it?"

But it wasn't anyone, of course. It was just the walkaway spell in the shoes sending them back to the two bad brownies.

The people of the village began to get very upset. Everyone who bought lovely new shoes from Slick and Sharpy lost them in the night. And then, when they brought their old shoes to be mended and took them home again, those went, too!

Slick and Sharpy just slipped walkaway spells in the mended shoes as well—and, of course, they walked away to the little toadstool house the very next night!

"Our money-box is full," said Slick. "Most

of the shoes we have made for the people here have come back to us—as well as a lot of their old shoes that we mended."

"Good," said Sharpy. "Let's go to another village now. We can settle in and do no work for a long time because we shall have so many pairs of boots and shoes to sell!"

"We'll just make this last pair of high boots for Mr. Bigfeet," said Slick. "He has promised us five gold pieces for them—so that means we will have a lot of money from him—and if we put the usual walkaway spell in the boots we shall have those, too, because they will come back to us to-night!"

Mr. Bigfeet called for the boots that afternoon and paid for them. "I hope no one comes to steal *these* boots!" he said. "They're beautiful!"

Now, Bigfeet had a little servant called Scurry-About. She was a timid little goblin, very fond of her big master. She thought the boots were lovely, and she polished them till they shone that night.

"Oh, Master!" she said. "I hope no one will steal them!"

"Well, see that they don't!" said Bigfeet and went up to bed. Scurry-About always slept down in the kitchen. The boots were there, too. She looked at them.

"Oh dear—I sleep so very soundly that if anyone comes to steal them I would never hear!" she said. "I know what I'll do! I'll go to sleep wearing them! Then if a robber comes he will have to pull them of my feet and I shall wake up and scream!"

Well, she curled herself up in her small bed with the big boots on her feet. They reached right up to her knees! She fell sound asleep.

And in the night the walkaway spell began to work! The boots wanted to walk back to Slick and Sharpy. But they couldn't, because Scurry-About was wearing them. They began to wriggle and struggle to get themselves off her feet.

She woke up at once. "Who's pulling off the boots? Master, Master, come quickly, someone is stealing your boots!" she cried.

Bigfeet woke up at once and came scrambling down to the kitchen. He was most surprised to

find Scurry-About wearing his boots. And dear
me, what was this? They leapt off her bed,
taking her with them—and then began to walk
to the window. Up to the sill they jumped,
and then tried to leap out.

But Scurry-About was still in them, and she
screamed because she was stuck halfway through
the window. "Help, help! The boots are
taking me away!"

And then Bigfeet suddenly knew what was
happening! "There's a spell in them!" he cried.
"A walkaway spell, put there by those tiresome
brownies—the rogues! Scurry-About, I'm going to open the window wide and let the boots
take you away with them—but I'll follow close
behind!"

"Oh, Master! Help me!" squealed poor
little Scurry-About, and woke up all the villagers around, so that they threw on their
dressing-gowns and came hurrying to see what
was happening.

Bigfeet opened his window wide. The boots
set off at top speed with Scurry-About's feet in
them, taking her along, too. Through the wood
and into the lane and down the street—and

right up to Toadstool Cottage went those big top-boots!

And there they kicked at the door to be let in. Scurry-About was crying, and Bigfeet was shouting in rage. All the other villagers were calling out in amazement.

"See! They are walking off to Slick and Sharpy! The wicked brownies! Wait till we get hold of them!"

Slick and Sharpy heard all this and they were very frightened. Slick peeped out of the window. When he saw such an angry crowd he was alarmed.

"Quick, Sharpy," he said. "We must get out of the back door as soon as we can. Don't wait for anything—not even the money-box!"

So they fled down the stairs and opened the back door quietly. Out they went into the night and nobody saw them go.

The top-boots kicked the door down and everyone went inside the house. Scurry-About pulled off the boots, crying.

"They've gone," said Bigfeet, looking all round.

"But they've left behind their money-box

full of money—and sacks full of the boots they made for us!" said Mr. Tiptap, emptying them out. "Aha! It's *our* money because we paid it out to them—and they're *our* boots because they were made for us. How well-off we are!"

Nobody knew where Slick and Sharpy went to, and nobody cared. The villagers kept the boots and shoes and gave little Scurry-About two beautiful pairs for herself.

As for the money, it is being spent on a birthday present for the little Prince of Dreamland, who is five years old next week—he is going to have a box of big wooden soldiers, who march away in rows—and then walk back again! You see, Bigfeet found the walkaway spell in a box at Toadstool Cottage—won't the little Prince be surprised!

Mr. Twiddle's Afternoon

"Goodbye, Twiddle dear," said Mrs. Twiddle, all dressed up in her best things. "I'm just off to the tea-party, and I shan't be back till half-past five. Take the laundry in if it comes—and do please let the cat in if it cries. It didn't have its breakfast, so it will be very, very hungry."

"Let it be hungry then," said Twiddle, who didn't like his wife's cat. "That cat's always hungry. It wouldn't matter too much if it ate its *own* food—but yesterday it got the kippers out of the larder, and the day before it——"

"Yes, yes, dear, I know all that," said Mrs. Twiddle. "But I still want it to be fed today if it cries to be let in. Now, Twiddle—if you don't PROMISE me to let the cat in when you hear it crying, I shan't go to my tea-party."

Mr. Twiddle patted his wife's plump shoulder. "Now, now—don't be silly. Of *course* I'll let the cat in, *and* give it food. You needn't worry, my love. I don't *like* your cat, but I'll be kind to it, I promise you."

Mrs. Twiddle went off happily. Twiddle

watched her out of the front gate, then he sat down with the newspaper. Ah—peace at last! He could really have a very, very long read.

"Yow-ee-ow! Yow-ee-ow-ee-ow!"

"Yes, you *would* come yowling at the back door, just as I sit down," said Twiddle, crossly. "All right, cat, I'm coming. I'll give you such a big dish of fish that you won't be able to meow or move for hours after you've eaten it."

He went to the back door and opened it. No cat walked in. "Come in," said Twiddle, impatiently. "Puss, puss! Come in, I say!"

No cat came in. Twiddle poked his head out of the door. He couldn't see the cat anywhere. "All right!" he said, "if you're going to be funny, you can *be* funny!"

He slammed the door and went back to his chair. But no sooner had he opened his paper again than he heard the yowling noise once more.

"Yow-ee-ow, ee-ow!"

"You can wait a bit this time," said Twiddle and he settled down to read. But the noise went on and on, and at last he could bear it no longer. He put his paper down and went to the back door. He flung it open and looked out.

"Will you come in, or won't you?" he said. But there was no cat there to come in. A surprised sparrow looked at him and flew away.

"Don't tell me *you* made a noise like a cat," said Twiddle to the sparrow. "Where is that yowling animal? I can hear it again!"

Twiddle decided that the cat must be at the front door, not the back. So he padded back into the kitchen and went into the hall. He opened the front door. Dear me, how astonishing—no cat there either!

Twiddle stood and listened. Yes—there was that horrid yowling again but it didn't sound quite so loud. Was the cat trying to get in at one of the windows?

He went indoors and upstairs. He opened all the windows and looked out—no cat anywhere at all! Twiddle began to feel very cross.

"Wasting my afternoon like this!" he grumbled. "I'm going down to my chair, and the cat can yell its head off for all I care! Anyway, it's stopped now."

He sat down again, and read half a page of his paper. And then the yowling began again,

this time even more loudly. Twiddle flung down his paper.

"All right! I hear you! For goodness' sake come in! Haven't I left the kitchen door open for you?"

But no cat came in at the door. Twiddle couldn't understand it. He began to feel quite worried. Was the cat trapped anywhere and couldn't get out? In the shed perhaps, or up in the roof? What *would* little Mrs. Twiddle say to him if she came home and found that the cat was locked in the shed and couldn't get out, and had been yowling all afternoon?

Twiddle sighed. He went to the shed and unlocked it. He spent quite a time peering here and there, and making nice catty noises, hoping that the cat would slink out, wherever it was hidden. But it didn't.

"It must be up on the roof then," said poor Twiddle. "That means a ladder. Now, where in the world is the ladder?"

He found it at last and climbed it carefully to the roof. But however lovingly he called, the cat didn't appear from behind any chimney. It was most peculiar.

The yowling went on. Mr. Twiddle simply *couldn't* decide exactly where it was coming from, and that made him quite certain that the cat must be trapped somewhere. He began to feel very hot and bothered.

"Puss, Puss, poor Puss!" he called. "Where are you? I've got fish for you, fish-fish-fish!"

The yowling stopped for a while. Then it suddenly began again, even more loudly. It seemed to come from the next-door garden. Twiddle peeped cautiously over the hedge. No cat was to be seen there at all.

"It's a puzzle," said Mr. Twiddle, scratching his head. "Oh my—look at my trousers! I must have got them dirty going up to the roof! Blow this cat. It always gets me into trouble."

Twiddle was so worried by now that he forgot all about his tea. He began to hunt everywhere for the cat. He looked in the dust-bin and in the greenhouse. He looked under the hedge and up all the trees. He looked into the coke-bin and into the coal-cellar, calling "Puss, Puss, Puss" all the time. Really, what *had* happened to that animal?

He crawled under the currant bushes, he went into the hen-house. He got hotter and hotter and dirtier and dirtier. Sometimes the yowling stopped and sometimes it went on. Twiddle began to feel that he was in a peculiarly disagreeable dream.

The front gate clicked. Twiddle rushed to see if the cat was coming in, but it was Mrs. Twiddle. She left the gate open and came down the front path. Twiddle met her at the door, and she stared at him in horror.

"Twiddle! What *have* you been doing? You are filthy dirty—your trousers are stained—your coat is torn—and your *hair*! It's standing straight up, and you really do look most peculiar."

"I *feel* peculiar," said Twiddle. "I've been hunting for your cat all the afternoon and I can't find her. She's been yowling and yowling and——"

"She *hasn't*, Twiddle," said Mrs. Twiddle. "Don't tell stories like that!"

"I tell you she has!" almost shouted Twiddle. "Why do you suppose I went hunting for her if I didn't hear her yowling? I've been up on the roof. I've been under the currant bushes. I've been . . . *ooooh*! Look there!"

Mrs. Twiddle looked behind her. Walking daintily in at the front gate was the cat! It walked right up to the door, slid in beside Twiddle and made its way to the kitchen, where it began to gobble the dish of fish.

"Where's it been?" asked Twiddle, weakly.

"I'll tell you," said Mrs. Twiddle. "When I went out this afternoon, the dear creature followed me. It followed me all the way to the bus-stop, and then I saw it! So I had to pick it

'up and take it with me! It's been with me all the afternoon—and came down the street after me just like a dog when I went home!"

Twiddle sat down suddenly on the hall chair. He couldn't make things out. "But—but I tell you it's been yowling all the afternoon," he said. "I heard it—yowl—yowl—yowl! That's why I looked for it."

"Twiddle, are you quite well?" asked Mrs. Twiddle anxiously. "Oh dear, how dirty you are! And really, there must be something the matter with your ears if you heard the cat yowling all the afternoon. She has certainly been out to tea with me!"

"I did hear it, I *did*," said poor Twiddle. Then he suddenly sat up straight. "Listen! It's yowling again!"

"That's not Puss yowling," said Mrs. Twiddle. "Look, there she is, eating her dinner. Not a yowl in her!"

"But listen! Don't you hear the noise?" cried Twiddle. "There it goes again; yow-yow-yow!"

Mrs. Twiddle listened. Then she began to laugh. She laughed and she laughed. She took

Twiddle to the back door and pointed to the garden next door.

"Oh, Twiddle, you'll be the death of me!" she said. "You really will! Look—what can you see on the lawn next door? Tell me."

"A pram," said Twiddle.

"And what do you suppose is inside the pram?" asked Mrs. Twiddle.

"A baby," said Twiddle, puzzled.

"Yes—and it's a *yowling* baby!" said Mrs. Twiddle. "Listen to it! Yow-ee-ow-ee-ow! Yow! Just like a cat. Oh, Twiddle, Twiddle—

you've been hunting a baby's howl all afternoon! Whatever *will* you do next?"

"Yow-ee-ow-ee-ow!" The baby next door wailed and rocked its pram to and fro. Yes, it sounded exactly like a cat. Mr. Twiddle felt suddenly very cross and very hungry.

"I'm not sitting here listening to babies yowling like cats," he said. "I'm off to get my tea at the tea-shop down the road!"

And off he went, slamming the door. He hadn't gone far when he heard a noise. "Yow-ee-ow!"

He turned round, and—bless us all—there was Mrs. Twiddle's cat following him! Yow-ee-ow!

"Clear off! Scat! Off with you! Grrrrrrr!" shouted Mr. Twiddle, much to the astonishment of all the passers-by. Poor old Twiddle—he does make things difficult for himself, doesn't he!